Servant to the Spidae

Aspect and Anchor

Book Four

Ruby Dixon

Copyright © 2023 by Ruby Dixon

All rights reserved.

No part of this book may be reproduced in any form or by any electronic or mechanical means, including information storage and retrieval systems, without written permission from the author, except for the use of brief quotations in a book review.

This book was not created with AI. I do not give permission for AI to train upon my work in any way.

Stock Photo: Depositphotos.com

Cover Design: Kati Wilde

Map: Mr. Ruby

Edits: Aquila Editing

Proofreading: Fortunate Books

❦ Created with Vellum

Servant to the Spidae

All my life I have served. One lord after another, I have given them my time, my body and my soul. My newest lord, however, is not one but *three*.

I have become the anchor to the three Aspects of Fate, the mortal chosen to teach the gods humanity. It seems an impossible task for any mortal to satisfy a god's wishes and I must serve *three*?

Three lords means three times the frustration, three times the petty demands...

...and three times the pleasure.

This book is exactly what it says on the box - one woman and three men. The streams do not cross but everything else is on the table. Enjoy!

Tower of the Spidae
Edge of the World
Ashen Deep
Godspine Mountains
NOVORO
YSHREM
Katharn
AVENTINE
Temple of Storms
Dirtlands
Sea of Storms
Tadekha's Citadel

A note about content

This book is full of spiders.

No, really. If you've read my prior books in this series, you will know that the gods of fate in this fantasy setting have spiderlike mannerisms. There are spiders in the tower. There are spiderwebs everywhere. This is the moment in which I need to tell you that if you are weirded or ooged out in any way by spiders, spiderwebs, pods, and the like, turn back now. It's not used in a horror-movie trope sort of way, but it is frequently brought up. Just warning you!

In addition to spiders, the book contains the following themes that might bother some readers:

SPOILERS AHOY!

— References to past sex work
    — References to past abuse and slavery
    — References to the death of a partner
    — Sexual encounters of a quid pro quo or 'servicing' nature (but consensual)

— Claustrophobia
— Isolation
— Concerns over abandonment

Enjoy...?

One

YULENNA

"I'll do it."

I say the words before I even know what I'm thinking. It's partially to stop Faith from arguing with the terrifying Fates—the Spidae—and partially because I see a path to safety ahead of me.

As a bed-slave, you learn to judge the world a little differently than most. You gauge every action by whether or not it will further your need for safety and protection. I've served in brothels and I've served fancy lords in the past, and I definitely know which one I prefer. Aron of the Cleaver, the Butcher God of Storms, was my protector for a time, but now he has Faith, and anyone can see that he'll never have use for someone like me again. I need a new master, one with enough power so that I'll never have to be on my knees in a brothel ever again.

And even though the Spidae terrify me, it's the perfect solution.

The two Spidae in the room arguing with Faith fix their gazes on me. It's like they're seeing me for the first time. I get that a lot around Faith. I've always been considered a very beautiful, desirable slave, but Faith has a brash, magnetic sort of personality that draws everyone in and makes them like her despite her crude words. Maybe it's that she's Aron's anchor, but there's an otherworldly sort of appeal to her that makes me invisible at her side.

Now that I've spoken up, though, I am invisible no longer.

The Spidae with pale eyes narrows his gaze at me, not moving, but I feel...dissected from the inside out. "An interesting thread," he murmurs.

"I see it now," his brother says, the one with vivid blue eyes. "Very interesting."

I don't know if this is good or bad, but they're looking at me now instead of Faith. They're judging whether or not I'd be a good toy for them. And if it's one thing I've learned, it's how to be the best kind of toy. So I lift my chin and give them both my best smile, one that gives just a hint of sultry teasing. I stand up straighter, knowing that my breasts will be prominent, and when I shift my hands on my skirts, I deliberately smooth the fabric so it emphasizes my small waist. "I will serve the gods."

"Wait, Yulenna, no. You don't have to do this." Faith frowns at me, stepping in front of me and grabbing me by the shoulders. She pulls me away from the two Spidae, who are watching me now with avaricious expressions that tell me I'd be serving in their beds before dark if they agree to take me on. I can handle it.

But Faith looks miserable at the thought, as if it's somehow her being roped into servitude.

It's both awfully sweet of her, and awfully frustrating. She truly has no idea what kind of position I'm in. "I know."

"You...you really want to serve them? An anchor has to go willingly," she asks, her voice frantic.

There's a movement behind her. A third Spidae enters the room, standing near his brothers. It's like they've all come to look at me and decide if they want me or not. He's got the same blank eyes his brothers do, maybe even more so. His eyes are shockingly dark in his pale face, like two pits, and it's jarring to look at, just like the hungry expression he wears. They're terrifying all together, all three of them, and I wonder if I'm going to have to bed them all three at the same time, or if they'll simply take turns.

I decide it doesn't matter. Serving a god—a trio of gods—would be the safest, most prestigious sort of servitude I could ask for. Even if they send me away, I'll be a woman who served *gods*. I'll never see a whorehouse again. It's absolutely a gamble I'm willing to make.

Faith notices the third Spidae enter, and I could swear she shudders. "You want to stay here? Really?"

Do I? She still doesn't get it. I'm bargaining for my future. But Faith has always been privileged with being Aron's anchor. I smile bravely at her, confessing the truth. "Not really. I'm kind of scared, actually. But if you can learn a new world, so can I."

"Yulenna, no, this is different—"

One of the Spidae is suddenly at my side. It's the one with pale eyes, the one who watches me with such fierce intensity it's as if he's trying to read my thoughts. He reaches out with one pale, long-fingered hand and touches my braid, stroking my hair. He's so close that he smells like cobwebs and dust, and I don't know what to make of that. "You would serve us in all ways?" he asks. "The three of us?"

I nod.

"Time out," Faith bellows, gesturing with her hands. "No. Absolutely not. Yulenna, you're not a whore any longer, okay? You don't have to do anything like this."

I shake my head, trying to look over at Faith even as the god plays with my hair, his fingers tracing over the ribbon I laced into my dark hair this morning. I always look as good as I can, because my value is in my appearance. I dress each morning knowing that Aron has forgotten about me, so I have to charm Solat, or Markos, or even the quiet Kerren into falling for me. If I'm married, after all, I don't have to return to the slave-yards. I deliberately wove that ribbon into my hair this morning because Solat said red looked good on me.

I wonder if the Spidae knows the meaning behind it as he

fiddles with my dark braid. He leans in, and I could swear he sniffs my hair. Goosebumps prickle over my skin, but I'm resolute. This is the best path for me. Like Faith, if I'm an anchor to a god (even a terrifying trio of gods), I'm safe from a life of drudgery.

And best of all, if I'm serving Fate, I won't meet the same terrible end that most anchors do.

"I want to do this, Faith," I tell her. She needs to understand. I meet her gaze, trying my best to ignore the god that hovers over me and strokes my hair so unnervingly. "Here, I have a purpose. I can serve the gods. Once we leave this tower, I'm just an unnecessary whore for a god who is in love with his anchor. I cannot fight in Aron's army. How long do you think he will keep me around?"

From the look of despair in Faith's eyes, I can tell she's starting to get it. She looks ready to cry. "You're my friend. Aron would keep you as long as I want. You've been good to me, and to him."

That's sweet of her, but friendship can only carry someone so far. I reach out and squeeze her hand, comforting her. "You have been my friend, too. Thank you for making me feel like your equal in all ways. But now I must find my own path."

She looks stricken, and I find it ironic that I'm comforting her even as I'm making the biggest decision of my life. Even now, my purpose seems to be to serve others. I bite back the stab of resentment that shoots through me, because Faith *has* been kind. She could have ordered me killed or sold off, but instead she's befriended me. It's not her fault that Aron fell in love with her. It's not her fault that I'm simply looking to secure my future. So I give her hand a little shake. "I can see the guilt on your face. Don't. I'm choosing this, just as you choose to be with Aron."

And I don't know if I'm convincing her or myself. Because the reality is that I'm utterly terrified…as much as I am resolute. I know this is the best path for me. A pretty face and a willing mouth only gets one so far, and both grow less appealing with age.

This is an opportunity not to be squandered.

Behind Faith, one of the Spidae extends his hand out to me in a silent invitation. The blue-eyed one. The dark-eyed one watches with a hungry, yearning sort of look, but he does not move, his hands tucked into his long sleeves. The other brother, the pale-eyed one, continues to toy with my braid, standing over me. I want to shout at him to step away, but one doesn't shout at the gods. And if I go into this, I belong to him.

"If you're sure," Faith begins.

"I'm sure," I say, my voice quavering. Am I trying to convince myself or her? But I take the pale hand extended out to me and step forward. The god's grip is feverishly warm, but he clasps my hand in his and it doesn't feel so terrible. We look like a study of contrast, he and I – me with dark, sun-warmed skin and chilled fingers, and him with burning skin and ice-cold looks. I say nothing as he draws me forward and then all three surround me.

I step forward into my new life.

Two

The tower swirls around me in a haze of mist, and my eyes unfocus. When they focus again, I'm in an entirely different place, a room covered in spiderwebs, but no door. There's no window, either. It's just shadowy and cool and remote.

A hint of terror curls in my belly.

The Spidae are still looming over me, the one toying with my braid as the other hovers far too close. The third one is behind me somewhere, but he's not touching me, and for that I'm absurdly grateful. I can't breathe. It's too much too quick, and the fear I've been fighting bursts into full-blown panic.

"I...I need to say goodbye," I blurt out. My thoughts have been so clouded and frantic with anxiety that I didn't realize until just now that I've forgotten to say my goodbyes to the others. "You didn't give me a chance."

The god playing with my braid pulls the ribbon free, loosening my hair. "Your life with them is over. You belong to us, now."

Of course I do. All my life, I've been traded as a commodity. I know how to cope with such sudden changes, too. I push aside my feelings, ingratiate myself with my new master, and handle it as best I can. But this isn't one new master, it's three. And it isn't a regular sort of slaver or a brothel owner who now controls my life.

It's a trio of gods.

I swallow hard, calming myself. They won't ask for anything I haven't given a dozen times over. All men and women are the same, when it comes down to reality. They want some touching and praise. They want to be made to feel powerful. I can give them those things. It's just...

I think of Faith and her acerbic comments to Aron, who greets them with amusement instead of anger. I think of her kindness to me. She could have sent me away a dozen times over in a fit of jealousy. I think of Aron, who isn't exactly kind, but who looked after me. He is a god, as well. He deserves a goodbye and my thanks. I think of Markos, who treated me like a lady even when he knew I was just a bed-slave. And I think of Solat, who has shining eyes and gentle hands, and has shared my bed recently, because I think I could get him to propose marriage to me and save me from a hellish future.

At the very least, I would like to let them know that they have been friends to me. "I would like to say goodbye if it's not too much trouble," I say again, keeping my voice as gentle and sweet as possible. "Please. It would mean a lot to me."

The hand petting my hair twists into it, and he forcibly turns me to look at him. Those too-pale eyes devour my face, and he looks furious. "Do you want to continue on Aron's quest or do you want to serve us? You cannot have both, female. Make your choice."

Something shrivels inside me at his rage. Already I've made him furious. "I want to serve you. I do. I'm sorry."

The blue-eyed one pushes his brother away. "Do not be jealous over her human lover, brother. That one has no future."

Did I think it was possible to get even more freaked out? "What do you mean, no future?"

Blue eyes turns to me, holding his hand out. "I will show you, if you wish, but you will not like it. Now. Will you be our anchor or must we search the threads for a more suitable candidate?" Behind him, the gray-eyed one gives me an icy look, while the other with the creepy, dark eyes just watches.

I'm dizzy with everything that's happening. It hasn't even been five minutes and my life has been upended. Do I serve these possessive, jealous gods, or do I continue on with Faith and Aron and the others? Solat has no future. If fate is telling me that, it means he will die soon. And while part of me cries out in despair, the larger part of me, the survival instinct, knows that it's just another path that I don't get to take.

The way ahead is with these gods, and the safety they offer.

Licking my lips, I take the hand extended out to me. "I'm sorry," I whisper. "I do want to be your anchor. This is just a lot of change. It takes a moment for me to work through it."

He nods, and his hand is hot against mine. "If you would tie yourself to us, know that this will be your home forevermore. We do not leave the confines of this tower. We also do not *share*. Is this understood?"

He's telling me that they live in lonely isolation here and that they're possessive...but I've figured that out already. Is he trying to scare me away? "I understand. I'll be yours."

Something hot crackles between our touch, and immediately, my knees go weak. His hand tightens on mine, and even as I sag in front of him, boneless and devoid of strength, he continues to clutch my hand.

"What does it feel like?" The gray-eyed one hisses to his brother.

"Pleasant," says the other god, and he sounds surprised, as if this didn't occur to him. "Like one thread is dedicated solely to you."

"Let me touch her," the gray eyed one insists.

The god with the blue eyes releases my hand and I collapse to the floor. Faith mentioned once that when she first touched hands with Aron, it felt like being struck by lightning. This isn't quite the same, but it feels intense and unsettling, like a heavy cloak is cast over me, draining my energy. It takes me a moment to realize I'm on my hands and knees in front of the three of them, weak and heaving.

When I look up, the gray-eyed one thrusts his hand out to me, almost as if in a challenge.

Somehow I know I have to touch each of them for this bond to work. I thought they were all the same, but the longer I'm around them, the less I think that is the case. So I somehow get to my feet again and stand straight, my hair sliding over my shoulders, unbound. I swallow hard and meet the silver gaze of the impatient, jealous one, and put my hand in his.

This time, his hand feels both hot and cold, like frost on fire. I shiver, waiting for the drain of energy, but it doesn't come. Instead, that strange *something* ripples all through me and finally stills.

"Hmm," is all he says to his brothers, his gaze thoughtful as he watches me.

I slide my hand out of his and turn to the third brother, the one with the hollow, too-dark eyes. Of the three, he's the most remote, and I extend my hand out to him. His nostrils flare and he gazes down at my palm with something like distaste. The god takes a deep breath, then grips my hand.

His touch is like ice.

To my surprise, the god moans unpleasantly. He immediately shakes my hand off, clenching and unclenching his fingers as if my touch has pained him. He withdraws a step or two, behind his brothers, and won't look at me anymore.

That was...unexpected.

"You are ours now," the gray-eyed one tells me, and his expression is one of triumph. "You will serve as our human anchor."

I nod, rattled. But I know my duties. "I am happy to serve, my lord."

"How long will you need?" Gray-eyes asks immediately.

I know exactly what he's referring to. He wants me to "serve" him sexually. To give myself to him. I knew this was part of the deal, but the fact that he's asking instead of demanding that I get on my knees tells me that I have a little opportunity here. Hunger rumbles in my gut. "I would like a bath and a meal first," I say. "Humans are fragile and I would go to you with my full strength."

He grunts. "I will return later, then." In a swirl of robes, he turns on his heel and melds into the spiderwebs covering the walls.

I blink in surprise, not entirely sure I didn't imagine that, and when I look over, the other two gods are gone as well.

I'm alone in this windowless, horrid room. Somewhere close by, I hear the sound of water turn on, likely a tub being filled. A knot forms in my throat, and I think of Solat, and Faith and Aron's easy relationship. I don't know what I expected, but this isn't it. I feel more like an object of curiosity than a person with feelings, and I wonder if I've made a mistake.

I think of Solat, and tears clog my throat. It's not that I'm in love with him. He was a good friend to me, and I wish I could tell him to be careful, that he might die. I wish that I had a window to the outside. I wish…

I swallow back my tears, because there's no point in crying. I'm used to slavery and servitude. This is no different than any other master, except now I serve the gods. There is honor in that, and I need to embrace it. So I push away my emotions, calm myself, and slip off my dress to go bathe.

Three

It seems even in a bath, I don't have the opportunity to be alone.

I lounge in the large, sunken marble tub (strange that a god would need one, but I'll take it) and stare off into the distance. I'm trying to mentally grasp everything that's happened. I'm an anchor now, like Faith. Unlike Faith, I feel completely and utterly out of control, and I'm wondering if I've made a mistake. Aron at least acts somewhat human. These three gods are terrifying in their strangeness. I can't help but think of how I touched the one's hand and he made a sound of pain, and backed away as if touching me was revolting.

Does that mean I am only serving two out of the three gods? I don't know and I feel like there's no way to get answers. I feel lost. It's usually fairly obvious what a new master wants from me. This feels a bit out of my depth, though.

So I sit in the tub until the water grows tepid and my fingers shrivel, my hair piled up atop my head so it doesn't get wet. I sit and I deal with my grief, grief that I won't ever see the outside world again, grief that I've left everything I know in exchange for safety and the honor of serving gods. I push the grief back down, because it serves no purpose, and focus on calming myself instead. As I do, I get the vague sensation that I'm being watched. I eye the walls around me, but I don't see any of the strange spiders creeping amongst the webs. I can't get over the feeling that someone's watching me, though. When I don't see anyone in the shadowy bathing room, though, I decide to take a chance. They're Fate, after all. Do they need to be present to "watch" me?

What is it they see when they look at me, I wonder? I know I am beautiful, with dark skin and dark eyes, full breasts and a rounded, enticing arse. My cheekbones are high, my chin pointed, and I have had poets exclaim over my graceful neck and shoulders. My hair is long and thick and I take great care to keep it shiny and curling, even though it takes a lot of time to tend to my mane. My eyebrows are perfectly shaped and my skin is supple and blemish-free.

Appearances are important for one in my position, and I've always done my best to ensure I am as appealing as possible. But do these gods even like dark skin and thick hair?

Do they notice such things at all?

Or am I just as strangely unappealing to them as their ghastly paleness is to me?

"You can show yourself," I call out, my curiosity getting the better of me."I'm not offended if you want to come and look." In a strange way, I'd be relieved. Being watched in my bath is familiar territory.

The webs part, and one of the Spidae materializes. It's like he appeared out of thin air, the webs molding to create the man who steps forward. I immediately search his gaze—blue eyes. In a way, I'm relieved. He seems the most rational of the triad, though I think the gray-eyed one takes the lead over the others.

He approaches in a way that is almost hesitant, as if he's not certain he should be here. I give him an encouraging smile, patting the edge of the tub. "Did you wish to see what I looked like naked?" I guess, trying to determine his thoughts. In a way, his mannerisms remind me of a master I once had, a virgin lordling who was uncertain in the bedroom due to his inexperience. "You but have to ask and I'm happy to let you look your fill."

"I know what you look like," he says. "I have seen the entirety of your thread."

I flinch at that. Of course. I'm still thinking that he's human in any way. That's my first mistake. "I did not mean to presume—"

"I am curious, though. Most females who are watched in a bath by an unknown male scream or are terrified. You show no fear, yet you did not know I was watching. Why is that?" He tilts his head, the movement jarring and inhuman in its jerky rapidity.

"Well," I say, sitting up in the water enough that my breasts rise from beneath the surface. His gaze goes there automatically, and that's a very human reaction. Hmm. I remember suddenly that they need an anchor because they lack humanity. They look human, they sound human, but in certain areas, they are clearly not human. Perhaps the bulk of my job will be to educate. "Unlike a lot of women, I have lived in servitude all my life. My body has been traded many times and I have no shame of nudity. There is nothing I have that belongs to me, even now."

The Spidae's head tilts again, his expression quizzical. He stands perfectly straight, his shoulders tense and his hands clasped behind his back as his long robes flow about his body. "You do not belong to yourself?"

"I am your anchor," I reply.

"Yes. But it is not slavery."

"Isn't it?" I offer him a smile to take the sting out of my words, drawing my knees up and hugging them. "I am yours now, to serve you in all ways. You'll forgive me if I don't see how that is all that different from slavery." I gesture at my surroundings. "I have been taken away from my friends and told my life will start over now. This has happened to me a great many times, each time I was sold to a new master."

"But you volunteered for this," the Spidae says, his voice stiff. "Thus it is not slavery."

"Servitude, then," I correct, resting my arms on my knees. "But you have seen my thread. Did you think I have a great many choices ahead of me?"

"I cannot see the future," he says. "My domain is the past."

"Ah." I pause, because this doesn't make sense to me. "Then how did you know about Solat's future?"

"My brother," he says, as if that explains everything.

It doesn't. It only leaves me with more questions, but it's clear this man—god—doesn't know how to answer them. It's another thing we'll have to work on, I guess. Patience, Yulenna, I remind myself. They have been gods for all eternity. It will take time for us to figure each other out. I open my mouth to ask another question and my stomach lets out a loud growl.

The Spidae blinks, his head cocking like a dog's. "That embarrasses you."

I grimace. "A little, yes."

"You are hungry." When I nod, he continues. "Why do you not eat?"

As if I've had a chance? It's been a whirlwind ever since the Spidae arrived in Faith's quarters and declared they needed an anchor of their own. I don't think my head has stopped spinning for a single moment, even though I know I've sat in this bath for at least an hour. There's too much up in the air for me to relax. But I gesture at the spiderweb-covered walls. "I know there is food in the pods, but I have no knife to open them. And it doesn't feel right to go around prying things down."

"Why not?"

"This doesn't feel like my home." I spread my hands in a helpless gesture. "You pulled me here and didn't allow me to get my things or visit my friends one last time. Now I'm in a chamber that has no windows or doors. It feels like a cage."

"But…it is safe."

"How safe do I need to be? Other than Aron's party, you're the only ones here!"

The Spidae blinks at this, as if it genuinely did not occur to him that I might not enjoy a room that's like a tomb. "You would prefer different quarters?"

"If it's not too much to ask, I would like a room with a window. I've always wanted one, and if I'm going to be spending the rest of my life here, I would love to have a view. As for a door… it's a necessity for me. I can't travel through spiderwebs like you can." I hesitate and then add, "Unless you want me in one room and only one room."

"This is your home now. You should come and go as you please."

It doesn't feel like my home. It doesn't feel friendly at all. But I manage a small smile at his polite offer. "Then will you show me around? How things are laid out? So I'm not afraid?"

He blinks, the movement slow and thoughtful and somehow meaningful, even as his body remains completely still. "I will escort you, yes."

I beam a smile at him. "Thank you. I would love that." I stand up in the tub, water cascading down my body, and hold a hand out, indicating he should hand me the towel waiting nearby.

The look he gives me is quizzical again, and it's clear he doesn't grasp what I'm asking for. He also can't take his eyes off my naked, wet body, and I suspect that seeing me in the flesh is very different than seeing me via my thread.

"My towel?" I ask sweetly. If I think of the three of them as untried virgins, then perhaps I can gain control of the situation. Perhaps I won't feel so lost if I have even the tiniest bit of power. As it is, I feel rudderless.

I can't even pray to the gods for guidance. They've all been cast down except for the Spidae, and I'm serving them.

The god picks up my towel and hands it to me, a curious expression on his face. He watches intently as I wrap it around my torso and step out of the tub. I loosen my hair, letting it cascade over my damp shoulders, and then begin to dry my limbs off. I lift one foot onto the edge of the tub and smooth the towel over my leg, glancing back at the Spidae. He hasn't moved from his spot, watching me with a fixed, burning gaze. "Do women ever come to this place?" I ask him.

"Rarely." He continues to stare at my leg. "Most of the supplicants we receive are of the male persuasion."

It makes sense. Women don't have the freedoms that men do. A woman traveler alone is nothing more than a target, and it occurs to me that if I ever wanted to leave, I'd be that lone woman traveler. Hot panic flashes through me, and then subsides again. I can't leave anyhow. I'm tied to them. Anchors endure unimaginable pain if separated from their aspect, and I have three aspects.

Even if I change my mind, I'm stranded here, so I have to make the best of it. I bite my lip, and then glance over at the man standing in my room. He seems to be fascinated with my bared limbs, and when he reaches out, I hold still. He only brushes a bead of water off my skin, though, and then rubs it between his fingers.

"Do gods bathe?" I ask, suddenly curious.

He shakes his head, a slight frown on his face. "Why would we?"

I shrug. "You have a tub here."

"It seemed like a thing to have," he comments. "I have seen them in mortal homes."

Ah. I wonder how much of what is here—the tower, the rooms—is mimicry without understanding. I suppose that's a question for another day. I towel my skin off and then pull my dress back on, tying the laces under the bosom to tighten everything back into place, and then slip my shoes on. "Sorry," I say as I turn back to him, realizing I've just made a god wait on me. "It takes a little time to get dressed."

He tilts his head. "You do not have to wear anything around us. No one is here to see."

"But I like dresses." I like the expensive fabrics, and the rustle of the clothing as it moves over my skin. I love pretty things, because I never had them as a child. "And I prefer walking around clothed. It feels too exposed to be naked." I lift one foot and gesture at it. "And I need these for my feet to protect them. Your floors are hard and cold."

He frowns down at the stone floors as if they suddenly offend him. "Do we need new ones?"

"Of course not." Just hearing him suggest that makes me vaguely anxious. "I don't want you to change anything for me. It's not my place. I can easily wear shoes." And I give him a sweet smile, sliding my hand into the crook of his arm. "Now, about that tour. You said you'd show me around my new home?"

The Spidae blinks, his gaze focused on my face as if he's momentarily dazzled. Perhaps he's not close to women very often, and I immediately wonder if I've made a mistake in grabbing his arm. He doesn't think like other men.

But then he puts his hand over mine, trapping it upon his arm. "Follow after me."

I hold onto his arm as he moves towards the wall, and when it's clear he's going to glide right on into the spiderwebs that cover everything, I squeeze my eyes shut and let him lead me. The webs brush gently over my skin as we walk forward, but I never feel the walls. When I open my eyes again, I'm inside what looks like a kitchen. There are far less cobwebs here, though everything is covered with a fine layer of dust. There's a large wooden table in the center of the room, a massive hearth, and a variety of pots and pans, along with a sink for washing vegetables...if there were any vegetables around. I blink in surprise, because I didn't realize there was a kitchen here. Our small party has been here for days and has eaten only what raw fruit and vegetables we could find in the pods, along with the occasional rabbit, cooked over Faith's fireplace. "Oh," I breathe. "This is unexpected."

"Is it? Why?" The Spidae looks at me curiously.

"I didn't think you would eat," I confess.

"We do not."

I gaze up at him, thoughtful. "Then why a kitchen?"

"For the same reason we have bathtubs and beds. Mortals

require them, and it seemed like something to have." He pauses and eyes me. "You need a kitchen, yes?"

My stomach growls again, and I nod. "If I'm to cook for myself, yes. Did you put this kitchen in for me?"

He shrugs.

Either he doesn't want to answer, or he's uncomfortable with what it is. Either way, I can take a hint. I release his arm and move through the kitchen, pulling open cabinets and the trap door that leads to a root cellar, looking at everything. It's a fine, large kitchen, as nice as anything in a castle, and I'm rather pleased by the sight of it. There's no foodstuffs, though. No cheese, no vegetables, no flour. The larder is completely bare, and I give a little sigh of disappointment. "Provided I ever find something to eat, this will come in handy. Thank you, my lord."

I'm already thinking of ways to organize things, and the entire place needs a dusting. The hearth needs wood for a fire, and there's a lot to be done. I haven't worked inside a kitchen for years, but I do know the basics. It's something to do, too, which I have to admit, I like the idea of. It's better than just sitting in my room staring at a wall all day long.

But my room has no doors, I'm reminded. I'll have to wait for one of the Spidae to bring me here. "You'll retrieve me from my chamber so I can come here regularly?" I ask the god standing nearby. "If it's too much trouble, perhaps I could settle a bed down here?"

"You will not," he tells me. "I want you safe, where no one can touch you but us."

Ah. I bite my lip, because the thought of being trapped in a windowless, doorless room for the rest of my days makes me die a little inside, but this is just a starting point, I remind myself. Just because it's my reality now doesn't mean it will be my reality always. So I put on a brilliant smile. "Whatever you say, my lord."

"You call me that, but I am no lord."

"I have nothing else to call you. Would you prefer, 'my god' or 'my Spidae'?"

His mouth flattens, his expression going vague as he considers this. "But I am one of three. I am not 'your' god or 'your Spidae' as this implies you only serve me."

"Perhaps we'll come up with something better after a time," I say brightly. "Unless you'll allow me to be so bold as to call you by your given name?"

"Given...name?"

Oh dear. Is this another "mortal" construct? "Yes. Like you call me Yulenna? That is my name."

"I have called you nothing yet."

I cringe inwardly. "Forgive me for misspeaking. I did not realize—"

"You are afraid of me." He tilts his head again and that frown grows broader. "Afraid of displeasing me. Have I been so monstrous to you, then?"

Panicked, I try to think of what he would want to hear. "You are a god," I manage. "My only job here is to please you. When I've said something wrong—"

"I did not say it displeased me. Just that I have not called you anything yet." His brows furrow. "Are mortals all this sensitive?"

I force myself to take a calm, controlled breath. "I'm just anxious, my lord...Fate." I add the title after I realize what I've done. "I truly do wish to please you."

"Because I could wipe you from existence as easily as waving a hand?"

I go utterly still, hardly daring to breathe. A cold sweat breaks out on my skin.

"I would not," he says in a low voice. "It serves me no purpose to acquire an Anchor and then simply destroy her."

I sink to my knees, wondering if it's too early to fellate him into liking me. Most men are more amenable after their cock has been thoroughly sucked. Getting eye-level with his belt should help indicate that I'm willing. "I want to please you. Just tell me what to do to make you happy, my lord Fate."

He frowns at me. "I don't like you shivering with fear."

"I shall try to be braver," I say eagerly.

"I would like for you to be yourself, I should think. I do not know how mortals act and I wish to observe you for a time." He continues to frown down at me. "Why are you on the floor?"

"I...wondered if I might suck your cock." I give him my brightest smile.

The Spidae blinks. "Why?"

Why? He honestly doesn't know why? Or is he toying with me? He's Fate, all-knowing and all-seeing. Surely he knows what sexual pleasure is. "Because it feels good?"

"Ah."

"Do you wish me to pleasure you?"

He thinks for a moment. "I will consider it. Are you not hungry?"

"My needs are nothing compared to yours," I tell him brightly. "I can eat later."

The look he gives me is downright withering, and I suspect he doesn't grasp my eagerness to please him. Either that, or it makes him suspicious. I'm just so anxious that I can't help myself. It's the former slave in me that's desperate to conform to a new master's wishes.

So I bite my lip and try again. "I *am* hungry."

He nods slowly, and I get the impression that my honesty pleased him more than my sniveling. "Then you must eat. And you must tell us when you have needs to be met. We have no such needs, and thus we will not realize when you need something from us. It will be up to you to speak when you are suffering. Do you understand?"

Chastised, I bow my head in acknowledgement. "I do. Thank you, my lord Fate."

The Spidae grunts. "I am not sure if I like Lord Fate as a title either. I suppose you must call me something." He lifts his shoulders in what must be the most awkward-looking shrug ever, and it's clear to me that he's mimicking yet again. "Wait here. I will bring you something."

I clasp my hands in front of me and do as I'm bid, watching him.

He doesn't move, and after a few silent moments pass, my skin prickles with unease. Did I misunderstand? Should I get my own food somehow? There's two doors in the kitchens, one heavy wood one that is sealed shut, a large copper pot placed on the floor in front of it. The other doorway is wide open and I see the slanted ramp of the stairwell that leads up into the rest of the tower. If I go up there, will I run into Faith and the others? The tower seems incredibly quiet, as if myself and the Spidae in front of me are the only people here.

Then, I hear something.

Scuttling.

The sound is faint, like something is brushing up against the webs, and the hairs on the back of my neck stand up. I get to my feet, instinctively moving closer to the Spidae. "Do you hear that?"

"Hear what?"

Before he can respond, one of the massive, silvery-pale spiders appears in the doorway to the tower. My throat turns into a knot and I cower behind the tall god, terrified as the many-legged creature moves into the room. It's the size of a woale calf, coming up to my waist, and the legs are long and stretch obscenely far. It fixes its horrible, dark eyes upon me for a moment, then it drops something on the floor and turns and leaves again, the webs rustling as it does.

"Do not be frightened of the spiders," the god at my side says. "They will not harm you. They are extensions of us."

"Y-you control them?" I cling to his sleeve, relieved he hasn't pushed me away. I stare after the terrifying creature as it retreats in a flurry of legs. Horrifying.

"Control? No. They are an extension of us." He shakes his head. "Like a hand, or a foot."

I stare at him, surprised. I don't entirely understand, but who am I to question the gods? "So if I see a spider, it's one of you?"

He inclines his head. "They will never harm you."

That makes me feel a lot better. I release his sleeve, and I'm chagrined to see that I've twisted the delicate fabric in my grasp. I smooth it out with my touch, biting back the apology that springs to mind. He doesn't want me constantly apologizing. He wants... well, I don't actually know what he wants. They've never had an anchor before, and I've never been one. We have to get used to each other. "I'm not always like this," I tell the Spidae in a soft voice. "I just need to get my bearings and then I won't be quite so..."

I don't know the word. Afraid? Timid? Frantic to please?

"I know," he says simply. "Eat your food."

When he doesn't move, I pick up the web-covered pod the spider laid on the floor nearby. I find a knife and carefully cut the pod open, finding fresh peaches. Ravenous, I grab one and bite into it, the juice dripping down my chin. I bite back a moan, devouring the fruit as quickly as I can, and then tearing into the next one. The rush of sweetness helps abate my hunger, but I pick up a third one and bite into it, famished. "Faith mentioned an anchor eats a great deal," I comment as he watches me eat. "I'm going to need more than fruit. Some meat. Eggs. Flour for bread, if you have it."

"I will see what I can do," he says. "For now, eat your fruit."

I cut off a slice and offer him a bite. "Would you like to taste?"

The Spidae's mouth curls with a hint of revulsion as he gazes down at the fruit. He stares at it for so long that I think he will refuse, but then he leans forward and takes the slice from my fingertips, his mouth grazing over my sticky skin.

I bite back a gasp, because I didn't expect that. It wasn't sexual. I don't think he knows how to be sexual, or is particularly interested in that. But his hot, wet mouth on my skin sears through my mind.

The Spidae chews, his mouth open and his jaw moves so awkwardly that I'd laugh if I wasn't terrified of his response. He looks as if he doesn't know what to do with it now that he has it in his mouth. "Good, right?" I cut myself another slice and chew it quickly, then swallow it and touch my peach-sticky fingers to my throat, reminding him of the next step.

He manages to swallow, a grimace on his face the entire time. "I did not enjoy that as much as you."

"But you tried it," I remind him. "It's good to try things that we're unfamiliar with, don't you think?"

"Why?"

"So you learn. So you grow as a person..." I trail off as I realize who I'm talking to. He's not going to grow as a person. He's a god. But he wants me to teach him about humans, right? Eating is one of the basic drives. So I cut another slice off of the divinely sweet peach and lick the juice off my fingers. "Mortals have to eat constantly. Might as well take pleasure in it."

"And do you like pleasure?" he asks, watching me lick my fingers.

"Of course I do." I give him my best coquettish smile.

In response, he stares at me, his eyes narrowing. I get the impression he knows I'm trying too hard with my answer, and he's displeased, but it's out there now. I can't change it. I manage a wider smile and keep eating.

"If you see one of the spiders in your room, tell it what food you would like, and it will bring it to you if at all possible," he tells me. "We are not used to permanent guests, so it will be a novel experience for all of us." His words are dry with a hint of amusement.

I choke on the slice of peach, my stomach tightening. Permanent guest. So it's not my home, then. I'm just a guest. It's their home and I'm just...visiting? But I keep smiling, because what else can I do?

Four

After I scarf down the peaches and wash my hands and face, he continues to show me around the tower. There's room after empty room as we head up the ramp that leads to the top of the tower. The tower itself seems divided into multiple rooms along the exterior wall of the tower, and only a few, circular rooms along the interior. I manage to peek inside one of the interior rooms, but it looks empty of everything but cobwebs. There are far more of the exterior rooms, though, and each has a bed and a window in it, along with other accoutrements. When we pause in one, I recognize the fireplace.

This was Faith's room, but it looks empty. Surely they haven't left so quickly? I glance over at my companion, but he's treating this particular room with the same bored disinterest that he treats all others. I have to ask, though. "Are they gone?"

He blinks at me. "Who?"

"Aron of the Cleaver and his anchor. His companions. This was one of the rooms they were staying in."

"Ah." The Spidae shrugs. "I've moved you to a different timeline. I thought we should have privacy while you get comfortable with serving us."

A different...timeline? "I see."

He must sense my disappointment, for he touches my arm. "Come. I will show you something you will enjoy."

"What is it?"

The god only smiles mysteriously and leads me further up the ramp. At the next landing, there's a mass of webs covering a rounded portal and the Spidae brushes his hand over it. The webs part, revealing an entryway into a large chamber. This one has another one of the windows with a view out to the waters, and a window seat that I immediately covet.

It's also full of trunks and bags of varying kinds.

I step inside, curious. There are wooden trunks of all kinds, some that look so old they might disintegrate at a touch, some with fresh, new-seeming wood. There's a bag made of tapestry, and another enormous satchel made of leather, along with a saddle and saddlebags in the corner. The saddle looks...primitive and old. The room itself is cluttered from wall to wall with the trunks, and everything is covered with more dust. I cross my arms over my chest and look at the god. "What is this place?"

He shrugs. "Sometimes we get visitors."

This surprises me. "And they leave their things behind?"

"Not all leave here alive."

Oh. The news shouldn't surprise me. The Spidae live in the most remote spot in the world, behind the Godspine Mountains and across the Ashen Sea. There are no civilizations out here, no friendly towns or even scattered outposts. Anyone that dies on this side of the mountains is just lost forever. I suppose the spiders bring their gear here, and the Spidae have no purpose for it, so it sits, eternally. "That's sad."

"Is it? Why?"

I know without looking over at him that he's cocking his head at me, trying to understand. "They clearly had something urgent to ask you. Whatever it was, they didn't get to live long enough to use what they learned."

"You are certain they asked us for good things, then? Things like how to save a child, or how to marry a lover betrothed to another?" There's a surprisingly cynical tone in his voice.

My question was foolish, then. Of course no one would travel so hard and so far for innocent questions. They are likely sought out by those that want power. Those that want nothing good for the everyday folk in this world. "Then these trunks are a bribe to you and your brothers? To get you to see something in their favor?"

"Does it matter? The owners are long gone, and anything in this room is yours."

I start, surprised. "Mine?"

"A god has no need for mortal trappings. Even now, we only wear robes because it offends mortal eyes to be greeted by naked gods."

I picture Faith's reaction to that and I giggle. For a woman who serves Aron in all ways, she is surprisingly prudish at times. I can only imagine the horror on her face if the Spidae were naked around her.

The god makes a startled sound.

I turn, looking over at him, to see his eyes are wide as he gazes upon me. "That laugh..."

"Yes?"

"I liked it. It was...genuine."

I manage a small smile. If he can tell what about my manner is real and what isn't, I guess I'd better be real with him. "It was."

"I should like it if you did that more often," he says in a low voice.

Swallowing hard, I nod. "I'll try. This has just been...difficult for me. At least, more difficult than I expected."

"Why?"

How do I explain that I thought they'd be more human? That when I committed myself, I didn't realize just how isolated I would be? I only thought of the glory in serving a god, the safety it would provide for my future. I'm safe, all right. Safe at the edge of the world, doomed to live the rest of my life in a windowless cell. "I don't think I realized fully what I was committing to."

"And now that you do, you have regrets?"

I consider this for a moment. Do I? My other option was to remain with Aron's party and hope I would not be captured or sold away once more. Aron is a god of war, and his anchor must die so he can ascend. Even at Faith's side, it wouldn't be safe. "I think I made a choice because I had to, but that doesn't mean I can't be afraid of what the choice means. It doesn't mean that it's a bad choice, just a little intimidating. It's just going to take some time to settle in. That's all."

He nods. "Do you wish to return to your quarters, then?"

I hesitate. I don't want to go back to that windowless room. It feels like a tomb, a cage, and I think that's part of what's making me anxious. He wants honest reactions from me, right? "I don't like my quarters," I blurt out. "At all."

The Spidae's perfect, beautiful face is blank. "It is safe there."

"It makes me feel like I'm trapped." I lick my lips, nervous. "Can't I just wander around for a bit? I'll stay out of your way. You can put me back in there when I need to sleep, but for now I'd like to keep exploring my home, if that's all right. And if there's anywhere you don't want me to go, I won't. I promise."

The god considers for a moment. "You would rather not be safe in your room? I thought you wished to be safe with us."

"I'm at the end of the world. I am the servant to three gods. How can I be any safer?"

I expect him to smile, but he only gives me another curious look and then nods. "Very well. I must return to my duties, but if you need anything, call for us. The spiders are always watching and will let us know."

I'm so relieved I break into a wide grin. I want to grab his hands and squeeze them tight, but I don't know if he'll appreciate that. So I clasp my hands tightly together in front of me. "Thank you so much, my lord Fate."

He stares at me for a moment longer, and then turns and

melds into the cobwebs on the wall. It doesn't even bother me this time, because I'm starting to get an inkling of how things work around here. The webs—the spiders—they're all tools of the gods and not to be afraid of. Spiderwebs cover everything because that's how they move about in their home.

I glance at my surroundings. Do I stay here or do I head back down to the kitchen and make myself something? If I can find some meat and vegetables, I'd love a thick, comforting soup. Just the thought of soup—and the process of making it—decides me. It'll give me something to do instead of staring at the walls. I head for the entryway to go back out into the hall, and as I do, I absently lift the lid of the trunk closest to me.

And pause.

It's full of fabrics.

I turn, my attention now fully on that trunk, and open the lid all the way. Sure enough, the trunk is full of bolt after bolt of rich brocades and expensive silks. It's a treasure trove of fabric, and the realization fills me with sheer joy. The god—the Spidae with the blue eyes—said I could have whatever I wanted in this room. I can make myself dresses.

I can make myself *dozens* of dresses.

Happiness bubbles inside me at the thought. I love pretty gowns, the more ornate the better. When I was a child, we had no coin, and I was envious of the lovely gowns the other girls my age wore. At one point, I was sold into slavery to a tailor and his wife, and I assisted in their shop and taught myself to copy the fancy fashions of the wealthy upon my own clothing. It was a nice time, I think wistfully, until I grew breasts and the tailor's roving eye turned to me. Then I was sold off, and, well, that was that.

But I like sewing. And here, there's no one to tell me that a slave can't have a dozen flounces upon her dress. There's no one to tell me that flashy ermine is inappropriate for one of my status. I finger a lovely red silk, imagining the skirts I can make with the wealth of fabric here, and I smile.

The gods must be looking out for me after all.

Five

Soup fixes everything.

Hours later, I've got a basket full of feathers plucked from a fat bird, and a full stomach. I worried that I'd made too much soup between the two pods I'd opened up, one with the fowl in it and the other full of root vegetables, but I've eaten every bite. I guess it's lucky that I'm ravenous as an anchor? There won't be much left over to waste.

With a full belly, I'm feeling much more at ease, too. I've had strange turns of events in my life in the past and I've managed to handle them. The Spidae can't be a worse master than some of the ones I've already had. As long as I make them happy, I should be fine. And if it's a bit quiet up here, well, I can surely keep busy with sewing and cooking for myself.

There are far worse fates out there.

I'm scrubbing the kitchen free of dust and humming an old Glistentide tune to myself when my skin prickles with awareness. Someone is standing behind me, and I turn around to see one of the Spidae. I wipe my hands off on my skirts (since I have no apron) and turn to him, lowering myself in a deep bow. "My lord Fate, how may I serve?"

"You are still down here."

I'm not sure if it's a statement or a question, and I straighten. When I look up, I realize that the man standing before me is not the blue-eyed Spidae from before. This one has silver eyes, and he watches me like a hawk watches prey. "I am," I say to him, keeping my tone even. "I wanted to make sure the room was clean before I left."

He glances around, then looks back at me. "It is clean now."

"So it is." The god seems to be waiting for something, and a ripple of awareness pricks at me. "Are you hungry, my lord Fate? Thirsty?"

"The gods do not have those needs." His silvery gaze glitters.

"Do you have...other needs?"

That gets his focus. He nods, almost imperceptibly. "I am curious."

I figured as much. I knew it was only a matter of time before one of them wanted to play with their new toy. But I've been in this sort of position before, and a body is just a body. So I give him a pleasant smile, hitch my skirts up to my waist, and bend over the large table in the center of the kitchen.

For a brief moment, I wonder if he'll be offended. If he wants me in a bed instead, or if he wants me to suck his cock. But then a hand touches my flank, and I figure I've chosen correctly. It's not about me. Never is. It's about trying out a new plaything. I think about the other Spidae, the one with the blue eyes, and how he didn't like my falsely bright smiles. No fake orgasms, then. I try to think if there would be some other sort of response that would please the god. Prayers? Supplication of some kind?

But then he's on me, his weight heavy against my thighs as he presses me against the table. For a moment, he fumbles against my cunt, prodding but not making any headway, and grunts with displeasure.

Right. "A moment, my lord Fate," I murmur. I lick my palm wetly, dragging my fingers in and out of my mouth until they're slick and dripping, and then reach down to my cunt, and shove my fingers inside. A moment later, he's there again, and this time he pushes into me.

My breath hitches at the size of him and the vaguely uncomfortable burn of his body as he thrusts into me, but that goes away quickly enough, and I lie still and quiet underneath him. He smells like dust, and he moves so hard and quick against me that his long hair teases my flanks. It's strange, though. He doesn't even grip my hips. He tries not to touch me at all, which is odd. The god grunts once again, and then something cold and wet floods my insides. That makes me squirm with a hint of surprise, but of course a god doesn't cum like other men. It's different, and I shouldn't be surprised.

"Thank you, my lord Fate," I murmur.

"Why are you thanking me?" His softening cock leaves my body and then his weight is gone.

"For honoring me," I reply automatically.

"Are you honored, then?" There's a hint of sarcasm in his voice.

Am I? In a way, I suppose I am. A god had sex with me. I've had two gods inside my body now—Aron and now this Spidae. It amuses me that I probably have the holiest cunt this side of Aventine. "A god's favor is always an honor," I admit, and it's the truth. When there's no response, I shake my skirts down and straighten, pushing off the table. I turn around and no one is there.

I'm in the room alone. Hmph.

For a god, the silver-eyed Spidae has terrible manners. The least he could do is give me a pat of approval...if he approves of me at all.

Something wet and sticky trails down the inside of my thigh, and his cum feels different than expected. I shove my hand under my skirts and touch my pussy, wiping away strands of his thick release. When I pull my hand back out and examine it, I see spiderwebs.

I can't decide if I'm revolted or amused.

A FEW DAYS PASS, AND THEY BEGIN TO FORM A PATTERN. When I wake up, one of the Spidae is there, watching me. Usually it's the blue-eyed one, as he seems more fascinated with me than the others. I lay on my back and let him use my body, staying quiet so I don't give him false responses, and he seems content to thrust into me a few times and then finishes.

It's not bad sex, but it's not good for me. Then again, no one ever truly tries to make it good for me, so it's not as if I'm surprised. After I clean up, Blue Eyes lets me out into the rest of the tower, and I spend my day cooking up meals for myself or digging around in the room of discards. I sew ornate dresses for myself. I make hand towels out of the cheapest-looking fabrics. I embroider a pretty apron. I gaze out the windows at my surroundings. I dust the kitchens and the room full of trunks, which I've come to think of as mine. I organize.

I keep myself busy, or I try to, at least. And I stay out of the way.

At some point during the day, the gray-eyed god will seek me out. I service him, too, and my sessions with him are as uninspiring as his brother. He waits for me to lick my hand, then pushes into me from behind and pumps a few times, and then disappears. He must be getting something out of it, I decide, as he seeks me out at least twice a day.

It's all very...tepid.

The Spidae haven't expressed disappointment in me, but I get the impression that something is off. It almost makes me feel like a child who has disappointed her parents, but I'm not entirely sure why. It doesn't feel as if they seek interaction with me? Beyond the first day when the blue-eyed Spidae showed me around, they haven't sought me out to speak with. They haven't had conversations with me. They just show up to get their dicks wet.

If that's all they want from an anchor, I suppose I can provide that.

But is this to be the rest of my life? Just a warm, occasional hole for a pair of gods that seem bored with everything? The dark-eyed one never comes to visit me. If anything, he's avoiding me. That bothers me, too. I'm supposed to be serving all three of them.

After a full week of this, I decide to do something about it.

It's a rainy day, with the sun hiding behind the clouds, and the view outside is nothing but gray. Gray skies. Gray water. Gray mountains. It's as distressingly gray as the interior of the tower and it sours my mood. I eat a piece of fruit while sitting on the counter in the kitchen, and eye the large wooden door. I suspect it leads outside, though I've never tried it. Where would I go? Even just walking around outside isn't necessarily safe. Vitar, one of Aron's men, died to a thing that lives in the lake.

But today, I consider it. I consider going outside just to see if the Spidae will chase me down and bring me back. At least then I'd get some attention.

I'm...bored.

It's pathetic. I'm as safe as could be. I have all the food I could want, all the pretty material to make myself dresses and all the time in the world. And I'm going mad after a week of this.

I finish my fruit and hop off the counter, washing my hands clean of sticky juice. If I'm unhappy with my situation, I need to change it. I keep thinking about the dark-eyed Spidae, and how he hasn't sought me out, not even once. Is he unhappy with my presence? Is he waiting for me to approach him? I decide I should find out.

So I finger-comb my hair into a semblance of normalcy, smooth my new dress that I've made for myself (a ruffled creation of a deep, luscious red, my favorite color) and head up the ramp, seeking him out. All is quiet, and there's no sign of the other Spidae, yet I get the sensation that they are here, somewhere. Or do they all fold into one another when I'm not around? They're one god, but three facets of him, and I still haven't entirely figured out how that works.

Then again, maybe it's not for me to know.

I pass by a few of the inner chambers, the ones that I've never been in. The blue-eyed Spidae told me to stay out of them when they were sealed off, and right now, their doors are covered with a heavy glut of webs. Inside, I hear a faint, humming music, but I know better than to touch something that I've been forbidden, so I keep on going. It's at the very, very top of the tower, when the ramp is so steep that I worry I'm going to slip and tumble all the way down to the base of the tower, that I find an open door.

Inside, one of the Spidae sits on the floor, cross-legged, surrounded by a mass of glowing red strands. They seem to emerge from the walls themselves, crisscrossing the entire room and taking up every bit of free space. I can't get to the god without touching the threads themselves, but that somehow seems wrong. As I gaze upon them, they seem to pulse and throb, as if attached to a beating heart. I look over at the god again, and his eyes are closed, his hands resting on his knees, his head tilted back. He seems to be in communion with the webs in some way, and I hate to interrupt.

Yet the door was open...

"M-my lord?" I call out. "May I join you?"

His eyes open, and I see the dark, unsettling gaze of the third Spidae. Somehow I knew it was him, but now I have confirmation, and I smile broadly at him.

He flinches at the sight of me.

Oh, dear. "Am I bothering you?"

The Spidae shakes his head and immediately he gets to his feet and the strange, reddish strands melt away. I jerk back in surprise, gasping as the room empties out. He approaches me, and as he does, I notice he won't look at me. He keeps his gaze averted, first to my dress, and then just anywhere else he can. "What is it you need?"

"I don't need anything," I confess. "I simply wished to talk to you."

"What about?"

I smile to take the sting from my words, lest he think I am pouting. "You've been avoiding me, my lord. I wondered if my presence offended you."

"Offends me? No. No offense." He blinks and then his gaze flicks around the room. "Happy. Very happy."

He...doesn't seem happy. His expression is distant, and he still won't look at me. "Is there anything I can do for you? To please you?"

I hold my hand out, and he shies away again, flinching backward. Oh. That's not good.

"Touching," he murmurs, looking anywhere but at me. "Too much touching. I don't like it...do I?" He makes a distressed sound in his throat. "You are always smiling at me, Yulenna."

I am? "Is that bad?" I ask. "Should I not smile at you, my lord?" After a moment, I realize he's called me by name. It's the first time any of them have. "You know my name?"

"Know everything about you," he murmurs, and the sound becomes curiously soft and affectionate. "My soft, sweet-smelling Yulenna." His gaze goes distant. "You always know how to make me smile. Even after centuries."

Centuries? I blink in surprise, because I just got here a few days ago with the others. "Do you see the future then, my lord?"

"What will be," he mutters. "What will be. What could be."

How fascinating. No wonder he seems disoriented. It must be confusing for him if he's seeing the future, even right now as he speaks to me. Centuries, though? Does he truly see me living at his side for centuries? Or is he simply seeing some other vision and interpreting it as me? Entirely possible, given that he won't look at me.

"Will you tell me more about what you see?" I ask him, keeping my voice gentle. "So I can understand?"

"I see everything," he says, lifting a hand. As he does, the red threads rise up out of the floor around us again, weaving their complex web. "All the fates of all in the world. What can be and what will be. A million futures, spread out before me." He twists his hand, making a fist, and then lowers it again. The strings vanish once more. "But it is all death."

I swallow hard at that, a knot forming in my throat. Death? As in, my death? Or everyone's death? "But you are Fate, right? Not the god of Death?" I thought that was Rhagos, but maybe mortals are wrong about that sort of thing.

"I see deaths. I see possible deaths. I see actual deaths," he continues. "I see the fate of every person that ever lived unspooling before me." His expression grows weary. "And I see them aging. I see them withering before my eyes. Everything withers."

Oh. I remember reaching for him and how he'd panicked. How he'd hated when I touched him. "Do you see me dying?"

He nods, gaze averted. "You rot before my eyes."

How horrible. "Is that why you don't want me to touch you? Or why you avoid me?"

The Fate says nothing, but I know the answer anyhow. It's obvious in the fragile set of his shoulders, the heartache written across his face. He's so different from the other aspects of his persona. Is it because he's the one that watches everyone die? No wonder the High Father split them.

I'm filled with curious sympathy and affection for him. He's obviously miserable, and I can only imagine what it does to his mind. "Is there some way I can make you feel better?"

"No touching," he says quickly, still not looking at me. "I cannot watch you wither. It hurts me too much." The god shudders violently, his hands covering his eyes. "Cannot watch the one I love age and die before me..."

Oh.

Oh. At some point in the future, he loves me? My heart warms for this strange, lost man. I want to pull him to my breast and stroke his hair, comforting him. I want to touch him all over and give him the affection he's clearly starving for. Why is it that the others are so detached when it comes to emotion and yet this one seem to be drowning in them?

I can feel just how lonely this Aspect of Fate is. It covers this chamber like a blanket. I sink to my knees in front of him, bowing my head. "I have given your other aspects comfort with my body," I say in a low voice. "Can I not do the same for you?"

He lets out a ragged, pained groan of need even as he turns away. "Cannot look upon you. Not like this."

Hmm. "Must you look?" I ask, curious. "What if you close your eyes, my lord?"

The god frowns mightily, and I cannot tell if he's annoyed by my words or confused by them. "My...eyes?"

"Yes. Close them tight," I instruct. "As if we are playing a game of hide and seek, like children do." The moment I say the words, I feel like a fool. He wouldn't know what children do. He has never been one. But maybe he has observed such things. "Have you seen children play such a game?" I prompt.

He continues to frown, and I feel foolish. Why in all the gods' names am I practically begging this man—this stranger—to allow me to suck his cock? It's ridiculous.

And yet...he clearly needs comfort and affection. And that is one of the things I truly excel at. Isn't that my job here, after all? To offer myself to the Spidae and bring them peace? I should have guessed that they would have no idea what my service would truly entail. Even though he's a god, I'm going to have to be the one that takes the lead. "Please close your eyes for me and keep them closed."

Uneasy at my request, it takes a moment for the Spidae to do as I ask. His eyes flutter closed and then he tilts his face up, as if that will somehow enable him to see.

Taking in a quick breath, I decide to take a chance. I reach for his hand and clasp it gently in mine. "How does this feel?"

His frown returns, and with it, confusion.

"Am I withering?" I ask. "Is my touch unpleasant?"

Realization crosses his face, and with it, wonder. "You..."

"Feel good?" I guess, when his voice trails off and pleasure lights up his features. Like this, with joy on his face, the god goes from cold and remote to astonishingly handsome. I can't help but smile in return, squeezing his hand. He practically clings to my fingers, clutching them in his grasp as if he doesn't want to let go of me, ever. I skim my free hand down his robe-clad thigh, still kneeling in front of him. "And does this touch please you?"

The god nods, still lost in the wonder of the moment.

I slide my fingers toward his groin, cupping him in my hand. "And does *this* touch please you?"

He groans my name. "Yulenna..."

I shiver at the way he says my name, so hungry and full of longing. It makes me want to do more. So much more. "Should I stop, my lord?" I whisper, leaning forward and mouthing his hardening length through his robes. "I am your servant. Command me at your will. My goal is to please you and nothing more."

"How?"

I love the hopeful note in his voice. This is where I can feel useful. This is where I can please my master. A curl of excitement unfurls in my belly, and I slide my hand up and down his thigh. "I can suck you." I lean in, nuzzling against the tent growing under his robes. "I can make you feel so good with just my mouth and tongue."

His breath catches, and I love how powerful it makes me feel.

"Would you like that?" I ask. "Or shall I leave you alone, my lord? Please tell me."

The god groans, and his free hand strokes over my cheek. "I would like this. I always like this."

I pull my hand from his grip and slip both of them under his robe. It's more voluminous than I realized, and after a moment's hesitation, I slip my head under as well. I feel a bit like a naughty child getting under his skirts, and the thought makes me grin. The view under here is rather impressive, I decide, running my fingers up his calves and then on to his thighs. His cock is enormous, as pale as the rest of him, but that's to be expected. He's a god. Of course he's going to have godlike equipment. His cock looks as if it's made of white marble, and he's hairless here, a long, thick vein stretching along the underside of his shaft. I grip him in my hand, hearing his breath catch, and then lick the prominent head.

The Spidae jerks in response.

"Is that all right?" I ask in a soft voice. "Should I stop?"

"No," he says quickly, shifting on his feet. "Do not stop. Keep—keep going."

"I'm just going to use my mouth and hands," I promise him, pressing a kiss to the twitching head of his cock. "My only goal is to give you pleasure." I press another kiss to his skin, and then, as I grip him tight, I kiss my way down his shaft, making sure each one is open mouthed and slightly lingering. By the time I flick my tongue against his sac, he's hard as iron in my grasp.

I move back to the head of him and give him another lingering kiss, and this time I flick my tongue over his skin. He twitches in my grip again, and I slide my hand to the base of his shaft, squeezing as I do. "If I had an oil, I could work you with my hands," I murmur as I lavish attention on him. "Just glide them over your cock and stroke you until you come. If you don't like my mouth, we can do that next time."

He grunts, and I have no idea if that's good or bad. It doesn't sound bad, though, and he doesn't ask me to stop, so I keep on going. I curl my tongue around him and then pull him into my mouth and suck. Two hard draws upon his cock and then he comes, spilling into my mouth and down my throat. At this point, I'm used to the web-like release and I swallow it all, licking his cock to clean him and then giving him one final kiss on the tip before I emerge from underneath his robes.

The entire chamber is now filled with webs, twice as much as before. I stifle a giggle at the sight and turn back to the Spidae.

The god still has his eyes closed, a look of surprised and delighted bliss on his face. I move forward and gently press a hand to his chest, letting him know of my presence. "Were my duties to your liking, my Lord Fate?"

He reaches for me, touching my cheek, and his thumb skims

over my mouth. "That was the best thing that has ever happened to me," he says in a low voice. "And I have lived a very, very long time."

I'm happy that he also sounds more...coherent than before. I press a kiss to his hand. "I'm glad I've pleased you."

"Very much." He strokes my face again. "I like touching you. I've never liked being touched before."

"Then you can touch me all you want. But I would advise you to keep your eyes closed," I tell him, sliding my hands over his chest and rubbing lightly. "If the sight of me affects your enjoyment, simply do not look."

"A simple but elegant solution."

That makes me smile, and I nudge my mouth against his hand so he feels it. "Mortals are very good at coming up with simple solutions, if not elegant ones."

He smiles back, and for the first time since I agreed to become the Spidae's anchor, I feel as if I've done my job. I've brought him comfort, even if for a few small minutes. My bringing him joy brings me joy, as well. I stroke his chest, since he seems to appreciate my touch. If he's not used to caresses, though, this might feel invasive for him. "Should I stop touching you? Are you uncomfortable?"

The god shakes his head. "I...like it." He almost sounds shy, and I can't help but notice that he keeps his eyes tightly shut, as if he wants this moment to go on between us, forever.

I'm in no hurry to wrap things up myself. My mouth tastes like cobwebs and musk, but it doesn't bother me as much as it did before. I run my hands over him, and as I do, I note the sparse room. "You need blankets and pillows in here, my lord."

"Why?"

"So we might lounge here and I can rub your shoulders, or your back, or anywhere else you might wish for me to rub," I say playfully, moving behind him and running my hand over his arms and down his spine. "Sometimes it's lovely to just lie about and cuddle."

"Do you have such things?" he asks. He tilts his head, inquisitive.

His reaction startles me. He is one of the triad of Fate, and a god. Shouldn't he have this answer? Is it because he sees the future? "You don't know?"

"I see nothing with my eyes closed," he murmurs, sounding fascinated. "Not even the future."

Oh. I press my cheek to his back and wrap my arms around him from behind. "I have them in my room, but I cannot get in there unless someone takes me...and I have no wish to go back right now." I love being touched and petted myself, so I can only imagine how good it must feel to someone touch-starved. I rub my nose into his back, noting that his long hair smells like dust. Everything in this tower smells like dust. I suppose I should press him to bathe, but that can wait for another day. Right now, this feels like a breakthrough and I'm content to live in the moment. "What should I call you?"

"Do you need to call me something?"

I run my hands over him again, pressing my breasts to his back. "If I touch myself to thoughts of you, I need a name to call you so that you know my words are for you."

The god groans, his head falling back against me, his hair cascading. "I have seen that before." He pants, and when my hand strays lower, I find that he's stirring again. I reach for his cock, teasing him into hardness again.

"You've seen that?"

"I've watched you," he admits. "So lovely. So sensual."

Interesting. "What did I call you?"

"Zaroun," he says in a dreamy voice. "You called me Zaroun."

I did? Oh, I like that. "It means 'dusk' in my mother's language," I tell him, pleased at my own cleverness.

"I know."

"Zaroun," I purr, working his cock. "Do you want me to make you come again?"

He shudders against me and nods.

Six

I stay with Zaroun for a long time, making him come twice more and then just stroking his hair as he lies on the floor and puts his head in my lap. It's the most satisfying afternoon I've had in a long time, and when he guiltily starts to glance over at the webs, I realize he needs to get back to work. Using the excuse of my growling stomach, I tell him I need to leave. He doesn't watch me as I go, but reaches for my hand, his face carefully turned away.

"You'll come back?" he asks.

"Tomorrow," I promise. "I'll come back tomorrow."

He doesn't respond to that, but it feels as if his fingers are reluctant to let mine go, and I leave his chambers with a smile on my face. I head back down to the kitchens, humming a Rastana tune to myself and dust my skirts off. For a tower that exists outside of time, how is it that there's so much dust on everything? It truly confounds the mind.

I wonder if Zaroun would let me dust his chamber for him, or if that's too pushy of me. I don't want the Spidae to feel as if I'm usurping their tower or their personal spaces, but at the same time, I want to make this more of a home. I want it to be more comfortable.

We'll all be more comfortable without dust on everything.

Before I can get very far, I feel a presence beside me as I move down the curving ramp that leads downward through the tower. Is it Zaroun, returning to my side? I look up—

—piercing gray eyes meet mine.

Ah.

I should have known. Of the three Spidae, the gray-eyed one seems to be the most dominant...and the most possessive. The look on his face is hard and slightly offended, his elegant nostrils flaring with distaste. "What did you do?"

I go still at his accusing tone, fear skittering up my spine. Have I offended one of them by showing preference? Did I do something wrong? "My lord? I do not understand."

His expression grows even more frustrated. "Why is it that around my brother you are all smiles, yet when I approach you show fear?" His tone changes, becoming vaguely petulant. "Why do you have no smiles for me?"

Blinking, I stand there in shock. "I-I didn't realize, my lord. I am happy to smile for you—"

The gray-eyed god waves a hand irritably. "Well, it's not the same if I demand it of you, now is it?"

He sounds like a jealous lover. Considering that the only thing I've done differently is touch his other aspect, I'm puzzled (and a tiny bit amused) at his reaction. "I am confused, my lord Fate. Am I not to serve all of you?"

"You are," he says, his tone full of ice. "But it is to be equal amongst us."

Is it not equal? Both the blue-eyed Spidae and the gray-eyed god before me now have used my body for their pleasure multiple times since I arrived. I don't see how me spending one afternoon with Zaroun—their dark-eyed aspect—will somehow skew things out of balance. "I'm afraid I don't understand—"

"You did something different," the Spidae accuses me, drawing himself up to his full height. "I can feel his mind, and it is no longer as wild as it normally is. He has contentment. Happiness. I want to know what it is you did to him." He leans in. "And why you favor him above myself."

I draw back as he looms over me. I'm genuinely confused now. "Why do you think I favor him more than you? Because I gave him a name? You asked for me to call you my lord Fate and I have done so faithfully."

His mouth purses and he gives me a hard look. "You pleasured him. With your mouth."

Oh. He's jealous of that? "I can do that for you too, of course. You simply have to ask." Even though we're standing in the hall, I sink to my knees in front of him and patiently wait for him to lift his robes. "I am at your service."

"But you reached for him," he says. "You reached for him and you smiled. You volunteered. You never volunteer for me. I do not understand what is different."

I reach for his robe, and he immediately grabs my wrist, his hand ice cold against my skin. "It is not the same, do you understand?"

Not the same because I had to be told? I wrench out of his grip, annoyed at his attitude. He's always been a bit difficult, but today it's really bothering me. I'm starting to feel more comfortable here in the tower, and maybe that's why I glare back up at him. "I know it's not the same. But you're not acting the same as he did, and so you get a different response."

That catches his attention. He circles around me as I get to my feet, and his gaze is intense as he watches me, so intense it feels like it's burning a hole into my clothing. "Yes. That's what I'm trying to say. Why is it that you are different with him than with me? Explain this to me so I might understand it."

Some of my anger fades at that. Of course he's confused. Hasn't he said that they need an anchor so they can learn how to be in touch with their humanity? He doesn't grasp the difference between my responses to him and to Zaroun. "It is different," I say as patiently as I can, "because I wanted to touch Zaroun. With mortals, there is a difference between submission and willing submission. I will give myself to you as many times a day as you ask, as often as you ask, but what you want cannot be forced. I touched Zaroun and gave him pleasure because he was sad, and because he was kind to me. I wanted to make him feel better, and when he had joy at my touch, I wanted to do more for him. You and your brother use me like you would a chamber pot, or a towel." I spread my hands. "I am not a person to you. I am an object, and so you can have me..." I gesture at the whole of my body. "But you cannot have *me*."

And I gesture at my heart.

He stares at me for so long that I worry I've offended him. I swallow hard and remain where I am, doing my best not to glare up at him. He's been arrogant and uncaring and I'm just now realizing how much I resented that. Aron—the old Aron, the Liar Aspect of Aron—treated me like I was nothing but a sleeve for his cock, a convenient cunt to plow and forget about. It wasn't until I saw him with Faith that I realized gods had feelings just like people, and they could care, just like people.

And now that I know that, I'm not going to settle for just being a cock-sleeve for the rest of my days.

"You would not touch me unless I demand it?" the Spidae asks, his voice silky-soft. "What if I demanded that you touch me of your own volition? Like you did to my brother?"

I shake my head. "You're still demanding it. The result is the same."

"How do I change the result?" He seems genuinely confused and as if he wishes to learn.

For a moment, I almost feel sorry for him. The god sounds depressed, as if he's realizing what his brother has is out of his reach. "There has to be emotion there. I have to want to touch you."

"So give me emotion. Make yourself want to touch me. Make yourself smile..." He pauses as he says the words. "It is not the same, because it is forced again." With a growl, he stalks away from me, heading down the ramp. "I hate this!"

He might hate it, but he doesn't ask for me to service him, either. Perhaps I've given him something to think about after all.

Seven

I don't get much sleep that night. Even though my quarters are empty of all but me, I can feel the Spidae's presence lurking just outside my room. He's there all night, and I can practically hear him thinking. He never comes in, and never says a word. Just lurks...and thinks.

And I know without asking which Spidae it is, too. It is the gray-eyed one, the one I've taken to calling "Neska" in my head. Zaroun is "dusk" in my homeland's language, because he sees all as it ends. I call the blue-eyed aspect Ossev, which is "dawn," or beginnings. But Neska?

Neska is what we call a troublemaker. Someone that is far too clever for their own good. It fits him and the way he studies me, like he's trying to figure out a particularly complex puzzle.

When morning comes, though, Neska's ominous presence is gone from outside my rooms. I suppose that's a blessing, but I'm not entirely sure what to think of it. Perhaps he's decided that pleasing me isn't worth the effort, and he can just go back to utilizing my body like he would any other pot or pan. Then again, I doubt he's ever used one of those, either.

I wash up and dress, and since my chambers are doorless, I'm forced to sit and wait for someone to come and retrieve me so I can eat something. Normally one of them checks in on me quickly, but today they must be ignoring me. I make a mental note to stash some food inside my rooms in the future just in case this happens again, and pick up my sewing.

I've just finished tacking on a ruffled sleeve when Zaroun enters my chambers, looking anywhere except at me. "You did not visit like you promised." His voice is low and vaguely sad. "Have I offended you?"

I set my sewing down and get to my feet. "Of course not. My room has no door and no window. I am kept here, caged, until one of you frees me, and cannot return until one of you brings me back. Have you forgotten?"

He gazes vaguely around him. "There should be a door here."

"You're a god. Make me a door, then," I tease, only half-serious.

"Yes, I can." He blinks, dark eyes unfocused, and then surges toward the wall. The stone ripples away from him, as if pushed away by an unseen force. I've never seen stone flow like water and my mouth drops open in shock.

It's a sobering reminder that I am a mere mortal serving gods, and that I should give them what they want.

"Come with me," Zaroun says, still not looking in my direction. He turns and leaves, heading deeper into the tower.

I put aside my sewing and follow after him. My stomach growls, but I ignore it. Now that I have a door, I can feed myself at any time. Tending to one of the gods comes first. The reminder of the door sends a little shiver of fear through me, because they're powerful and I'm not. I've been getting too comfortable. I need to treat them with respect and give them everything and anything they ask for.

We head to Zaroun's chamber, the same one we were in yesterday. The blankets and pillows are still there and he immediately sinks down into them, his eyes closed. "Blindfold me this time? I want to be comfortable with you."

My heart squeezes painfully at the intense need on his face.

For all that he's a god, Zaroun is so very lonely. How do the other aspects, the other fates, not see this? Or is this something that he only allows me to see? I think back to Aron and when I served him. Both his Liar Aspect and the Arrogance Aspect were very closed off to me. He only truly opened up to Faith.

But Faith was different. The way she talked, the way she considered things...all very different. I'm not like her.

"You are quiet," Zaroun says, eyes still patiently closed as he turns towards me. "Do you wish to be elsewhere?"

Oh. "I'm here," I tell him, and reach out to caress his cheek. His skin is cool against my touch, but when I caress him, a look of pure ecstasy crosses his face. The pure joy my touch gives him makes me ache, and I need to focus on the here and now. Zaroun wants my attention. "My apologies. I was just lost in thought."

"I know what it is like to be lost inside your own mind." Is that a tease in his voice?

I pull off the sash at my waist to use as a blindfold.. "Lean in," I tell him. "And then we can enjoy ourselves without fear."

Zaroun and I spend hours on the blankets together. My stomach eventually stops growling and I make a mental note to raid the kitchen later. For now, spending time with the Aspect is my priority. Today, he doesn't want to be serviced, though. He's content for me to stroke his hair as he lays his head in my lap, and I tell him about nothing at all. He likes the sound of my voice, and the feel of my hands, and so I share stories about the low, flat buildings in Rastana that are made of fired brick, and how they're carefully stacked atop one another like layer cakes. I tell him about how bright the sun is there, and how blue the waters of the sea. I talk of the bright fabrics from home, and how one of my masters was a silk-seller who had the most gorgeous bolts of fabric in jewel tones of every color, and how I'd loved to see them and touch them.

And all the while, I stroke his hair and touch his face, careful to avoid the blindfold.

It's nice. I'm not used to talking so much about myself, but I'm discovering that I don't mind it. Zaroun is a good listener, and he's content to hear me talk about anything and everything. There's no expectations, and it's just a lazy, sweet day.

Eventually though, he sighs. "I should return to my duties."

"If you need me, you know where I am." I smile at him as he gets to his feet. I get up, too, shaking out my skirts. "I'm going to go and get something to eat, but if you want me to come back later, just say the word. I'm happy to sit in the corner and sew if you want company."

"I shall think upon it." He takes my hand and lifts it to his mouth, pressing his lips to my knuckles. "My thanks, Yulenna."

My name. It shouldn't be so startling to hear coming from a god's lips, but I like hearing it. "You're welcome, Zaroun."

"Now please leave so I do not watch you die," he says, tugging at the blindfold that covers his eyes.

I quickly exit his chamber and head down the long, winding slope that encircles the tower. At the very bottom is the kitchens, and food, and my stomach growls as if in reminder.

Before I get very far, however, another figure appears. It's the gray-eyed Aspect—Neska. His expression is cool and hard, and I startle, moving aside. The smell of dust that accompanies him fills my nostrils. "My lord," I breathe, dropping into a curtsy. "Can I help you?"

"I don't know yet." He continues to regard me with that hard, vaguely displeased look, and I'm reminded of the fact that he waited outside of my room all night. He's probably spied on my time with Zaroun and decided that he didn't like it.

I don't know how I'm supposed to juggle pleasing all three of them if spending time with one annoys another. Biting back my frustration, I wait for him to say something. When he doesn't, I gesture at the hall. "I'm heading to the kitchens but that can wait—"

"No. Continue."

Oh. Very well. I pick up my skirts and head down the hall again, deeply aware of his stare boring into the back of my neck. He follows after me, a few paces behind, but says nothing. I can't help but feel that I've done something to offend him, but I don't ask what.

As soon as we get into the kitchens, though, he speaks. "I've decided you should service me."

I bite the inside of my cheek. Service him. Of course that's what he wants. That's all he ever wants. I remind myself that despite the pleasant time I spent with Zaroun, I must be mindful that all three of them are gods and all-powerful. That being with them here is an honor. Have I not served worse?

Dutifully, I haul my skirts up and lean over the nearest table. I push my bare ass out and spread my legs, waiting.

Nothing happens. He doesn't touch me.

A long, uncomfortable moment passes, and then I turn to look over at him. He's still staring at me with that hard look of distaste on his face. His robes remain closed, and I can't see if he's hard or not.

"Is this not what you want?" I ask. He's taken me like this many times before, so I know he doesn't mind the position.

"I am not hard for this."

His words are ice cold, as if I've done something wrong. Alarmed, I turn and drop to my knees in front of him on the floor. "I can service you with my mouth, or my hands, until you're hard—"

With an irritable flick, he pushes me away. "I want what Zaroun has."

Now I'm getting frustrated. "I have serviced Zaroun with my mouth—"

"That's not what I meant." He sounds petulant. "You smiled when you touched him. You made sounds of pleasure. I could *hear* them."

"Do...you want me to make sounds for you?"

"I want your pleasure!" He snarls at me. When I flinch backward, he sighs, the sound one of pure irritation. "And now you're crawling like you're terrified."

"You asked for submission. I'm giving you submission," I whisper. "I can't give you emotion unless it's earned...unless you want me to fake it."

Neska's lip curls. "The thought of you faking it is more offensive than the thought of mounting you right now. Why is this so unpleasant for me and so pleasant for Zaroun? What is the difference between us?"

He sounds genuinely bewildered, some of the anger leaving his tone. I pause, and then get to my feet, feeling as if I'm about to poke the beast. "The difference is emotion."

"You have said that before. I want your emotion if it makes such a difference." Neska's cold eyes burn into mine. "Give me your pleasure."

For a moment, I consider faking it and seeing if he notices the difference. His displeasure is a little terrifying to see, and the submissive slave I once was is far too used to doing anything to appease an angry master. "You can't turn it off and on like a faucet. Emotion has to be won. It has to be pulled forth."

"How do I pull it forth, then?" Neska's tone is no longer that of a spoiled child, but full of genuine curiosity.

"Well." I shake my skirts out, ignoring the rumble in my stomach. "You could spend time with me. Get to know me. Perhaps you could court me."

The moment the words leave my throat, they feel like too much. *Court* me? When I'm here to serve him? It's the most ridiculous thing I've ever said.

But he seems intrigued. "Court you? How does one court a mortal?"

"By doing things that will please me. Things that will make me feel affection for you. It's the affection that brings the emotion."

His eyes narrow with cunning. "What sorts of things?"

I eye him, and the scent of dust continues to tickle my nose. "For starters, I think you should take a bath."

He regards me. "A bath."

"Yes."

"I am a god-aspect. I do not sweat. I do not have the bodily functions that a mortal does."

You still come like one, I want to point out, but even that isn't quite the same. How many times have I cleaned spiderweb out from my cunt instead of seed drippings? "Nevertheless, I would like it."

"Why?"

"Because it would make me happy."

This time, his lip curls. "Why does my bathing have anything to do with your contentment?"

I shrug. "Why is it so important that I show real pleasure in your touch? I can fake it, like I said." I bite my lip and let my eyes go half-closed, my breathing hitching. I let it stutter as if I've just been caressed by a lover, and make a soft sound in my throat. It's the same thing I used to do with Liar Aron, who probably knew that I was faking it and liked it anyhow.

But the look on Neska's face is one of utter disgust. "That's worse than no emotion at all."

"Tell me what you want, then. I'm trying to please you." The worry starts to return. If he's not happy with me, what then? If only one of the aspects likes me, do I get sent away? Replaced? I've nowhere to go.

He pinches the spot between his brows and for a moment, seems completely and wholly human in his annoyance. "I know you are trying to please me. That is what makes this so very frustrating. I do not understand any of this. I do not understand why dunking myself in water will make you full of soft noises and real smiles. I do not understand why mad Zaroun pleases you more than myself. I do not understand this 'courting' or why it is required."

"Well..." I consider for a moment. "You are master of the

threads. You said they show you everything, right? Can you not watch other human lives and see what they do when they court?"

It seems logical to me, but he turns the suggestion away with a shake of his head and begins to pace. "Watching without understanding has been the problem all along. I can watch a carpenter make a house and not know how to build one myself. I can watch a weaver make a tapestry and not have the skills myself. Just because I see something play out in front of me does not mean anything other than the fact that I have simply seen it. *That* is the problem. I see all and understand *nothing*."

"And you don't know how to be human," I point out softly. That's why I'm here, isn't it? To help them figure out how to touch their humanity. It's more out of reach than I realized.

The arrogant look returns to Neska's face and he straightens his shoulders, gazing down at me with an imperious look. "I have never wanted to be human."

"What about your brothers?" At his puzzled look, I add, "The other aspects? Zaroun? Ossev?"

"Dawn. Hmm. Fitting." He pauses for a moment at the names I've given them, then shakes his head. "They are not my brothers. They are me, split into three pieces, just as Aron was not quite whole when he was split into his different aspects. We are connected more than Aron was with his aspects—I can feel what Zaroun feels. I can feel Ossev's thoughts and they can feel mine. We are connected…and so I know what I am missing when you spread your legs for me and your mind is distant." The look he gives me is accusing, as if this is somehow my fault.

I don't understand their connection, but I suppose I don't have to. He's a god, after all, and I'm just a mortal. But I understand jealousy. I smile. "So you're jealous of…yourself?"

He doesn't smile back.

I suspect my comment has hit the mark in a painful way. Is jealousy something that he normally feels? Something tells me that he doesn't feel much at all in any way, and so this must be a very uncomfortable emotion to experience. For a moment, I feel pity for Neska. What must it be like to be alone in this dusty tower, seeing the lives of mortals and not understanding why it is they act the way they do? It must feel isolating. He mentioned the three of them are connected, aspects of one another, but I don't think it's the same as having company.

Perhaps that's why Neska seeks me out so often. He's lonely and doesn't know how to handle it.

I'm far too soft-hearted, but I hold a hand out to Neska anyhow. "Come with me."

He frowns at me, gazing down at my hand, as if I've just asked a question he doesn't understand.

I wait patiently, not explaining myself. If he wants more from me, he's going to have to give a little. When I don't speak up, he stares down at my hand and then slowly puts his long, many-fingered one into mine.

It's a start, and I'm pleased.

I take his hand and lead him back up the long, cobweb-strewn ramp.

"Where are we going?" There's a hint of curiosity in his voice, and I wonder that he can't just read my mind—or my thread—and automatically know the answer.

"I'm going to bathe you."

He absorbs this. "Because it pleases you?"

"Yes, that's right. Because it pleases me. Do you object?"

"No." Neska sounds more intrigued than annoyed.

We're both quiet as we walk up the ramp, my skirts slithering against the webs. I see a spider or two scuttle along the walls, as if they're watching this development with interest, but no one interrupts us. Neska doesn't comment on the fact that I now have an opening into my rooms, either. He's silent as I draw him into my quarters and then turn on the water for my tub, waiting for it to heat. When it warms a bit, I add a drop of one of my favorite fragrant oils and then turn to him. "May I undress you, my lord?"

He gives me a sharp nod, his eerie eyes fixed on me.

I run my hands over the front of his robe, looking for fastenings. I'm not entirely surprised to find none save a small knot-and-loop tucked near one hip that functions as a button. I ease the strange, unearthly fabric free and realize this is the first time I'm going to see him naked. I've serviced him with my body, felt his cock a dozen different ways as he rammed into me, but this is the first time I've been able to explore on my own. Even when I touched Zaroun, his robes covered his body, protecting it from my gaze.

I wonder what a god looks like.

My answer is obvious—Neska is tall, slim, and pale. His limbs are not the graceful strength I expected, but an unnerving sort of willowy that I would associate with spider legs. His chest is slim to the point of skinny, his shoulders broad and adding to the vaguely gaunt look of him. It makes his erect cock all the more obscene, because it's the only part of him that seems thick and filled out, and flushed a startling pink against the deathly pale skin.

"I am not a god of beauty," he says suddenly. My staring must have gotten to him.

"No," I agree. "You are a god of time and fate, yes? I imagine appearances don't matter much to you."

"Should they?"

I consider this. "No. Appearances wither and fade. It's the spirit that is important."

He says nothing to that, but I don't sense disapproval with my words. He remains still as I tug the robes from his arms and fold them, setting them on a stool next to the tub. His hair is long, sweeping to the backs of his buttocks, and as gossamer and pale as the spiderwebs that cover the tower. I run my fingers through a few strands and I'm not surprised to find them as soft as they look.

Rolling my sleeves up, I dip a hand into the tub to test the heat, and when I'm satisfied, I turn back to Neska. "In, please, my lord."

He lifts one leg and picks his way carefully into the tub. The way he moves, I'm reminded of spiders again. But just like the spiders that lurk in the shadows of the halls, I'm no longer terrified of them. They're just different than me. And Neska seems strangely vulnerable in this moment, giving himself over to my care.

I like that. It makes me feel powerful. I lean over the tub and fix my gaze on him. "I'm going to bathe you now, my lord."

He nods.

Using one of my clips, I pull his silky hair up into a knot atop his head. "I'll wash your hair for you later," I tell him. When there's no protest, I wet a soft towel and add soap to it, then lean in and begin to rub it over his shoulders.

He makes no reaction to my touch, but I'd have to be blind not to see the thick log of his cock in the water. The tip is just barely brushing against the surface, that same lurid pink of arousal as I saw before. He stares straight ahead, and I can't tell if he's getting pleasure from my touch or simply enduring me.

So I lean in and make sure to brush my tits against his back as I stroke the cloth down his front.

That gets a reaction. He quivers, his entire body jerking, but he continues to stare straight ahead.

"Does my touch displease you, my lord?" I keep my voice soft and low, reaching over him to wash his shoulder. As I do, my breasts push into his face. "Should I stop?"

"No."

The word is soft, but it's enough. I continue to bathe him, pressing my breasts into his face at every opportunity. I bathe his shoulders thoroughly, and then slide the cloth over his thin chest and down his stomach. His cock is painfully engorged, and I work the cloth lower, wondering at my next step. Should I...?

I decide that yes, yes I should. Not just because I think he will like it, but because it'll please me to do so. I move to the little table I keep beside the tub and add a few drops of oil to my hand. I set the cloth down and then smooth my palms together. Leaning over the side of the tub, my breasts practically spill out of my gown when I move in, and I notice his gaze goes there. He's so busy staring at my cleavage that when I touch his cock, it catches him unawares.

Neska gives another full-body shudder as I close my fingers around him.

"Should I stop, my lord?" I meet his gaze, trying to keep mine unconfrontational. This is about me showing him what pleasure really is when it's given, not taken.

"...No."

Again, that one simple word. But I smile at him to let him know that I've got him, and I slide my fingers around his engorged shaft. With wet, quick strokes, I jerk him off under the water, my gaze on his face the entire time. I get to see every reaction, from the clench of his jaw as he tries to remain motionless, to the way his lips part and his breath quickens when my hand does. He gives the smallest shudder when he comes, but he grips my wrist when he does, and when I try to pull away, he holds me there, as if he needs me to keep touching him. I murmur soft words of encouragement, of how lovely his cock is, how much bathing him pleases me, of how much I liked watching him come, and I could swear that he enjoys my words as much as my touch. When he's done, I clean up the strange, floating clump of spiderweb that is his release and go back to bathing him. I wash his arms and move down to his fingers, massaging as I do. I move to his legs, starting with his feet and his long toes, and by the time I make it back up to his thighs, I can see he's hard again.

Neska is silent throughout this, but this time when I reach for his cock, he makes a soft little groan, as if this is a pleasure he didn't dare ask for.

I jerk him off again, clean the water of his leavings, and then wash his long, silky hair for him. I rinse it with fresh water, then run a bit of oil over my fingers and work it through the strands, detangling them. When his mane is combed out, I work it into a loose braid and then impulsively slide my arms around his wet neck, hugging him from behind because I'm so very pleased with this moment. It was just a bath, but it feels like more.

It feels like Neska is starting to see me, in a strange sort of way. So I kiss his cheek and whisper, "Now you don't smell like dust, my lord."

He turns to look at me, and the expression on his face is utterly dazed. I realize he's still pleasure-drunk from the hand-jobs I've given him, and it takes everything I have not to laugh with delighted amusement. Instead, I move to his ear and brush my lips over it. "Sex is just sex, but if there's an emotional connection, it's so much more, don't you think? I touched you today because I wanted to. Think on how it compares to how we touched in the past."

And then I pat his shoulder and get to my feet, the front of my dress wet and my skirts damp, and head down to the kitchens to get myself something to eat.

I'm feeling rather smugly pleased with myself. Let Neska mull that over for a bit. Let him think about how it feels when he's used compared to how it is when a touch is freely given.

I wake up the next morning to find Ossev leaning over my bed, his blue eyes vivid. "Will you bathe me?"

And I bite back a chuckle.

Eight

After the bathing incidents, things seem to change between us. The unspoken tension is gone. No one demands to be serviced or for me to flip my skirt up so they can fuck me. Instead, Neska and Ossev seem to retreat a step, as if content to wait for my affections to come naturally. Zaroun wants nothing more than affection and loving touches, so it's easy to spend time with him. Now, when someone seeks me out, it no longer feels like a chore.

Living in the tower has started to become…enjoyable.

Zaroun and I make time to spend together every afternoon, with his head in my lap and just caressing and petting. We talk of nothing, but our time together seems to calm him. He gets a bath, too, and even though no one seems to want to bathe themselves, at least the stench of dust is gone. I braid Zaroun's hair into intricate woven tails, and work on making a robe for him with a dark, embroidered trim to match his eyes.

Ossev is a simple one to please, too. He comes to me when I'm in the kitchens and asks questions about what I'm doing, what my plans are for the day, and what my food tastes like. He's fascinated with everything, and so I try to describe each bite or action, thinking of what Neska told me in the past—that just because they see what is happening does not mean they comprehend it. If I mention I miss a particular fruit, or a flower, I'll see a spider a few days later with a bundle for me, and know that Ossev is wooing me in his strange way with gifts.

Neska is the tricky one. He watches me at all times, sometimes, I suspect, even when I'm with the others. He does not ask anything of me. He doesn't give me gifts. He simply observes with narrowed eyes, as if I'm a fly he hasn't figured out how to swat just yet.

I try not to let it bother me.

Instead, I focus on making the tower my home, since I will be spending the rest of my days here. Ossev added a second door to my chamber, and a window. It is now light and airy, with a fresh breeze coming in whenever I like. It makes me feel less trapped to sit in the sunlight, and I love it. Now that I have a door and can leave whenever I please, I explore the tower a bit more. There's a few additional chambers like mine—with doors, of course—like the one Faith and Aron stayed in. I leave those rooms alone since they don't feel like they're used unless there's a visitor...and something tells me that even if there is one, I'm not going to be allowed near them. The Spidae are oddly possessive. I sweep the floor of the ramp clean of cobwebs, apologizing to the spiders as I do. I leave the walls alone, since I know they like to crawl all over them. I tidy the kitchen and spend a lot of time there, baking and cooking for myself. I'm dreadful at both, but I don't mind it, even when my creations don't turn out so well. I've only myself to please, after all.

The door to the outside is barred, and I haven't asked to go out yet. I'm not a prisoner, but something tells me that they wouldn't like me going out, either. It's too early for me to push my boundaries with the three Spidae more than I already have, so I keep my rooms tidy and try not to think beyond the walls here.

"Bread is supposed to rise," I tell Ossev as I work my dough on the counter. "I'm not sure why mine isn't. I think bakers normally let theirs sit in the sunlight, but I don't have a window down here." I slap the dough down on the surface again, annoyed. It has the right sort of consistency for bread, I think, but it's utterly flat. "Perhaps I should just make crisps instead of trying to make a loaf."

"Crisps?" he asks, leaning in to stare at my wad of dough. He's fascinated by baking and eating, perhaps because the Spidae do neither.

I nod. "Crisps are thin wedges that are baked. They snap and crack when you bend them. Bread is more pliable...and I wanted bread." I turn the dough ball with my hands again and then pause, considering it. "Maybe if I add some seeds."

"Why would you add seeds?" He reaches out one spidery finger and touches the dough, then rubs his fingertip thoughtfully. "It's wet."

"It is wet," I agree. "Maybe that's the problem. Maybe..."

I trail off because a shadow looms in the doorway. Neska is there, and his eyes narrow at the sight of myself and Ossev.

"You've been here long enough," Neska says, stepping into the room. "Your duties await."

With a guilty look at me, Ossev retreats and slides backward into the webbing that covers the wall, disappearing. No doubt he's reappearing upstairs in his chamber.

I smack the dough again, imagining it to be Neska's sour face. "That was rude of you."

"He neglects his duties. *Our* duties. We all have tasks we must accomplish, and we cannot afford to be distracted away from our work. Certainly not by a pretty face."

"So you think I'm pretty?" I'm determined not to get offended by him. He doesn't know how to be around people, and definitely not around women he likes. That much is plainly obvious.

Neska is silent, and I wonder if I've embarrassed him.

I glance up at him. He's frowning down at me. His gaze flicks to my limp dough, then back to my face. "Come with me."

Curious, I wipe my hands on a towel and follow after him. We start to head up the ramp, but then he makes an irritated noise and pauses, turning and offering his hand. I immediately take it, and in the next moment, our environment changes. I gasp at the sight of the room—Neska's room—filled with glowing strands that crisscross every bit of space.

He leads me forward, his touch delicate but strong. "Touch nothing. It could have consequences."

"Consequences? That sounds worrying."

Neska does not reply to that. He releases my hand and steps forward into the snarl of threads, somehow managing to avoid touching any of them. I remain where I am, watching. He lifts a hand, and his long, strange fingers dance through the threads, flicking and sorting through them as if looking for something specific. He moves faster and faster, his hands working at a speed that makes them blur before my eyes.

"Ah."

He pauses, running a finger along the back of one particular thread as if plucking it from its environs, and turns towards me. "Here."

Cautious, I step forward. "What is it?"

"A baker." His tone is carefully neutral. "He makes bread about this time every day. I thought perhaps if you saw his actions, you might understand why yours is not the same."

His words are vaguely insulting, but it's the actions behind them that touch my heart. Neska has seen my frustration and wants to help. It doesn't matter that he doesn't know how to pose it. I smile at him, thrilled, and move to his side. "Truly? Thank you."

"As I have said before, touch nothing." He gives me a sharp look, his finger still on the thread, holding it captive so it cannot sink back into the web of its brethren.

I glance up at him. He's trying so hard to be sour and failing miserably. His actions have said everything. "Can I hold onto you?" I slide my arms around his free one, smiling up at him. "If not, I'll back away."

He doesn't touch me...but he doesn't tell me to leave, either. Instead, he pulls the thread in. "Can you see it?"

"I can see the thread and your hand...but nothing else?"

Neska thinks for a moment, then traces a finger in the air. A mirror appears, floating in midair, and I gasp at the sight. I'm reminded again that he is a god and can create—or destroy—at a whim. The glass shows me against Neska's side, and I have to admit that we look good together. Him so ethereal and tall, and me, vibrant with curves. I am warm brown skin enrobed in a rich, fanciful gown, with as many pleats in the sleeves as my long hair has curls. At my side, Neska is all smooth, colorless mane and equally colorless robe.

The mirror's surface ripples, and then it's like we're looking into a bakery. Neska picks up the thread again, and pulls it toward the mirror as if anchoring it there. "Better?"

I stare at the images playing in the mirror. There's a man in there, of middle age with ruddy skin. He has loaves laid out in neat rows on racks behind him, and in front of him is a flour-dusted table. Off to one side, a large brick oven glows. It looks so real that I could reach out and touch it. "How did you...is this real?"

"It is real. You are seeing a hint of what I see when I touch a thread. This man owns a bakery. Perhaps by observing him, it will help you with your breads."

"Thank you so much, my lord. I love this."

I'm silent as we watch the baker as he works. He uses a scoop to add flour to a bowl, and then water, and something from a jar. He adds salt and a few drops of oil, and then begins to work the paste into a ball, slapping it before putting a towel over the bowl and pushing it aside.

"What was that in the jar?" I ask, looking up at Neska in disappointment. "I don't know what it was."

He shrugs, his shoulders fluid. "We shall have to watch more."

We continue to watch the mirror, and even though another bowl of ingredients is made—this time with herbs added to it—I still don't know what's in the jar. I crane my head as we watch the baker's movements, as if that will somehow help me understand what he's doing. But when he turns back to the racks of bread behind him, I realize that the demonstration is done for now. Disappointed, I turn back to Neska. "I'm understanding your frustration now. Just because you see someone do something doesn't mean that it's explained. There could be anything in that jar."

He nods, gazing down at me. "I will keep an eye on this thread for you. If he mentions it in passing, I will make note of it."

I give his arm a squeeze. "Thank you." I turn to the mirror, watching as the stranger continues to work in the bakery. "You can watch multiple strands at once?"

"Hundreds."

Hundreds? My stars. I rub his arm in sympathy, imagining the headache that must be. "Doesn't that get exhausting?"

The look on his face grows puzzled, as if he's never considered this. "Perhaps this is why the High Father wished for us to have an anchor. To ease us."

I feel a little guilty at that, because I haven't been doing a lot of easing lately. I think the High Father would probably want me as enthusiastic as Neska and Ossev do, though. I rub Neska's arm again. "I really appreciate you showing me this. It's helped me understand a lot."

"But not bread."

"No, not bread." I glance up at him, smiling. Was that a joke? It almost sounded like a joke.

"You may keep the mirror," he says, lifting a finger and tracing it around the edges of the glass. "I will have it placed into your quarters. If you wish to see something, all you need to do is ask to look at it, and your request will come to me."

Again, my jaw drops. He's going to let me snoop on whoever I want? That feels…naughty and exciting all at once. "Really?"

"I would not lie."

"I know. I just—" I look over at the mirror when there's a flash of motion, and to my surprise, a woman enters the bakery kitchen. She pulls on an apron and marches towards the man covered in flour. He stops what he's doing and tilts his head, and the woman kisses him. It's a quick kiss, once, twice, and they're clearly familiar with one another. Then, the man pauses, gazes at the woman, and they kiss again…this time, deeper.

I peek up at Neska and he's watching with utter fascination. Surely he's watched people kiss before? I'd wager anything that he's watched them fuck, too. Perhaps this is another one of those "can't comprehend" moments. When he looks down at me, his gaze moves to my mouth, his expression thoughtful.

Well now, this I know how to do. "Do you want to kiss me?"

"I don't understand the meaning behind it. Pressing mouths seems…wet."

"Your bath was wet and you enjoyed that," I point out, running a finger along his arm.

He makes a sound that might be annoyance, might be agreement.

"Kissing is sharing an intimacy with your partner," I tell him. "It's mouths and tongues meeting to taste and pleasure one another. In a way, it's a bit like having sex."

Neska eyes me thoughtfully. "And you like kissing."

It's a statement, not a question. "I have in the past."

"But not all kisses."

"No, not all kisses. Some are not given with the intent of pleasure. Some are not given at all." I shrug. "But a willing kiss with the intention of sharing something with a partner you care for? Those are lovely. Tender. Sweet. Very enjoyable."

"Then I want to kiss." He gestures at me as if I should take command. "Show me how it is done."

"Well, you're taller than me." I slide a hand up to the neck of his robe and give it a gentle tug. "You'll have to bend down."

A flicker of annoyance crosses his face, as if he doesn't like the thought of bending for anyone.

"Or we could go into my rooms and both of us sit on the bed, side by side, and kiss there." I tug his collar again. "But as we are, my mouth can't reach you. I don't know if you have noticed, but you are very tall, my lord."

Neska blinks, digesting this. "So I am." He slides an arm around my shoulders and pulls me in, and threads swirl around us, along with the air. The world seems to tilt around me.

A moment later, everything calms and we're back in my chambers, Neska having maneuvered us there. He flicks a finger and points at one of the cobweb-covered walls, and the mirror settles itself there. Satisfied, he turns back to me and waits, a hint of challenge on his face.

Right. I take his hand and lead him over to my bed, settling on the edge of it. He sits down, bending awkwardly as if he doesn't usually do such things, and looks wildly uncomfortable. His expression hardens and something tells me he feels vulnerable—and doesn't like it.

"May I sit in your lap?" I ask suddenly. We'll no longer be on equal ground—I'll be at his mercy. But perhaps that's what he needs for our first kiss. Perhaps he needs to feel as if he's in control.

Neska gives me a stiff nod, and I get up and move into his arms, settling myself on his knee. His leg feels thin under my backside, but I tell myself that he's a god and I'm not too heavy for him, no matter how willowy his frame.

Once I'm settled against him, I wrap my arms around his neck. "May I kiss you? If you don't like it, all you have to do is tap my arm and I'll stop."

He gives me the tiniest of nods, his expression tense. He's acting as if I'm about to attack him, not kiss him, but I'm starting to get a better grasp on Neska and how he thinks. He doesn't like to feel vulnerable. Where Ossev is more open to things, and Zaroun trusts me completely, Neska is suspicious. He sees malicious intent where there is none. Perhaps it has something to do with the nature of their particular tasks, but whatever it is, I know Neska is the one I must be the most careful with.

I lean in and ever-so-lightly brush my lips against his. His mouth is a hard, tight seam that offers me no give, and it's like kissing marble. I persist, pressing small, slow kisses to his mouth until he softens against me. I brush my nose against his and kiss his upper lip, letting my tongue tease against it, and I'm rewarded with a tremor going through his body.

Maybe Neska is so suspicious and cold because he feels more than the others and he doesn't know how to cope. Maybe being the Spidae of the present is the most draining, and so Neska must work that much harder to keep himself together.

I keep kissing him as if we have all the time in the world. I press my mouth to his over and over again, covering every bit of skin with sweet, gentle kisses, and occasionally letting my tongue flicker against his skin to keep him guessing. I slide a hand into his soft, gossamer hair and hold onto him, and this time, I let my tongue flick against the once-tight seam of his mouth.

I'm rewarded with the barest parting of his lips. Then, his tongue brushes against mine, and I'm the one shivering. It's just a light caress, but it's enough to feel tender and cautious, and how long has it been since any lover was cautious with me? As if I'm a piece of prized glass that must be cherished instead of someone there simply for their convenience?

Then, Neska deepens the kiss. I'm no longer the one in charge. His tongue lazily plays against mine, toying with me and teasing with light flicks. I'm no longer the teacher, and I don't mind. He's picked this up very quickly, and by the time he releases me, I'm breathless and panting, my body throbbing in response.

He regards me with that cool gray gaze, saying nothing.

It's like the tables have been turned and I'm now the vulnerable one. I breathe hard on his lap, my mouth tender and puffy from our kisses. "Did you like that?"

Neska's eyes narrow.

I suspect he's not going to answer me. If he says yes, he's giving me power over him. If he says no, I'm going to kiss him again, or worse—kiss his brothers. I can practically see the gears turning in his mind, weighing his options.

So I decide to see for myself. I brush a hand over his cock, and yes, yes he did like that. He's rigid under his robes, for all that he keeps his expression casual.

Neska grabs my wrist, pulling my hand off of him. He lifts it into the air, giving me an angry, indignant stare.

Perhaps I've pushed him too far. "I'm not laughing at you," I say softly. "I'm trying to judge what pleases you so we don't go down the wrong path. Not everyone likes kissing. There's no sense in spending time on it if you don't enjoy it."

He releases me and then gets to his feet so abruptly that I have to scramble to keep my balance. I tumble off his lap, staggering to my feet, and watch as Neska leaves my quarters in a swirl of long, silken hair and pale robes.

Nine

"He liked it," Ossev says, showing up at my doorstep later. He steps inside, not bothering to ask permission.

I look up at him, trying to hide my frown. I've been lost in thought all afternoon, wondering if I've angered Fate—a god himself—and now I'm going to suffer the consequences. I've polished and dusted my new mirror, hanging it back on the magical spot Neska had set it at and then stared at the shiny surface, wondering if kissing a god was so wrong.

And now Ossev is here. "What are you talking about?"

"Neska. You. Kisses. He liked it. He doesn't know how to say he liked it, but I can feel it through our connection. He's been thinking about your mouth all day instead of the mortals he's supposed to be watching."

Oh. That pleases me more than it probably should. I move over to my bed, sitting on the edge and adjusting my skirts. There is only one chair in my room and I figure I should leave that for Ossev. "Is that going to cause problems for Neska? If he's not paying attention to his work?"

Ossev shrugs. He moves to sit next to me, so close that his leg touches mine. He always does. I should tell him that I need room to breathe, but it reminds me that he's trying very hard for my sake, even if he doesn't understand human things like personal space. So I say nothing and smile at him. "Neska gave me a mirror."

"I saw." He watches me closely. "You like it?"

"I do. I like the thought of being able to look at things. It's more entertaining than staring at the walls."

"It's taking a piece of his power to keep it going for you. Every time you access it to view something, it will be like sending a request to him. He must like you a great deal if he made such an offer." He says the words with a hint of wonder, as if he doesn't quite believe it himself.

"You like me, and you're him." I give him a smile.

"Not quite. We are and are not the same." With that enigmatic answer, he tilts his head. "Shall I do the same for you? Give you the ability to see anything in the past?"

I blink at the gift offering. I'm not sure if this is out of competition with himself—Neska—or if there's a higher purpose behind it. "I wouldn't presume to ask for such a thing. You need your power and your focus, do you not?"

"But you are my anchor. I can learn from you by what you wish to see. It will help me understand you more." He reaches out to touch me, and then draws his hand back. "It is something that would give me pleasure, to know that I am entertaining you."

"Well then, how can I refuse?" I take his hand in mine. It feels cold against my skin, but they all do. It's like they don't know how to be a functioning, living person. That they're just pretending, like mummers on a stage. All the while, I'm acutely aware that they have all the power and I do not. "I should like it, Ossev, but I admit I don't know what I would look at. I want to check in on Faith and Solat and the others I traveled with, but beyond that..." I spread my other hand. "I can't think of anything to see that has happened in the past."

"Wars? The last Anticipation? The arrival of a great hero?" he suggests.

None of those things sound appealing to me. They're all the past, and they don't affect me.

"What about your birth?" he prompts. "You can watch when you came into being."

I shudder at the thought. "That's...disturbing. No thank you."

"Curious." His gaze grows sly. "What about Alothan? Would you like to see what happened to him after you parted ways?"

I tense, a knot forming in my throat. Alothan was two masters ago, and the worst one. He made me work in a whorehouse for pennies and whipped me when I wasn't obedient enough. He felt I was getting "used up" at the ripe age of twenty and sold me to another man, where I served in his house (and his bed) for four years before I met Aron of the Cleaver. The fact that Ossev has plucked that particular tidbit from my past tells me that he's been spying on my history. He should know how I feel. "I don't want to think about Alothan at all."

"What if I told you he died violently?"

"Good." My voice is flat.

"It was interesting. Are you sure you don't want to see?" Ossev leans in, his face practically in mine as if he's peering at my expressions.

"I do not." I get up and cross the room to get my sewing basket. If we're going to continue to talk of such disturbing things, I'm going to need something to occupy my hands. They always give away what I'm truly thinking, as if the anxious feelings inside me need to flutter out via my busy fingers.

Ossev frowns. "You're upset. But you have not seen him for years. Why does this upset you?"

"Because you are bringing up part of my past that makes me sad. That was a hurtful, awful time and I don't want to think about it, because it brings up the memories of pain. Do you understand?"

"I'm not sure." He moves to my side, stopping me when I

pick up the basket. Bright blue eyes meet mine. "I...did not wish to cause you pain. I do not like when you suffer."

He seems genuinely distressed that he's upset me, and I reach out to touch his cheek. He leans into my caress as if addicted, his eyes closing. "I thank you for your apology. I know you didn't mean to harm me. But not every experience is a good one, and if I dwelled on those times, I would never smile. Do you understand?"

"I do, and I would rather see you smile." He brushes his lips against my palm. "Just let me ask one final thing. If you could pick his fate, this Alothan, what would you have had done to him?"

My mouth curls in a wry smile as I consider this. "Something painful. A quick, easy murder would be too good for him. I'd want him covered in honey and eaten alive by rats, I think."

Ossev's eyes widen and a startled laugh barks from him. "You are supposed to teach us to be human, Yulenna!"

"Cruelty is very human." I lower my hand out of his grip and shake my head, setting my sewing basket on the corner of the bed. "If someone enslaves you and abuses you, I don't see how they merit anything but hate."

"Do you hate us?"

I turn to face him. "I don't know. Am I a slave here?"

The sharp edge in my voice surprises him. I can see it in the look on his face. "You are not a slave. You are an anchor. You serve us."

"But I'm not free to go, either." I gesture at the floor, indicating the kitchens below. "You've locked me inside. That makes me feel like a trapped slave."

He blinks, gazing at me. He stares at me for so long that I worry I've said too much. "You want to go outside? Why?"

"Just because I can. Just to breathe fresh air. Just to know that I can leave if I wanted to. Staying because you wish to stay is a different feeling than staying because there's no way out. Do you understand?"

"Not entirely," he admits. "But if it means a great deal to you, then I will take you outside."

He moves to take me in his arms, and my heart sinks, because I know what will happen. He will whisk me outside in a flurry of cobwebs and then whisk me back inside, and I'll still be as trapped as ever. I put a hand on his chest, stopping him. "I want a door," I say gently. "One that is available at all times, like the one to my room."

"But you are safest enclosed in the tower with us."

"Ossev?"

"Yes?"

"Are you a god?"

"Yes."

"Then you can protect me."

He blinks again, digesting this, then nods. "I will...take you outside. With a door."

"Thank you."

I can tell he doesn't entirely understand, but he's desperate to please me. Perhaps I'm pushing too hard, but after the memories of Alothan, all I can think about is how desperately I wanted to escape him for all those long years. How I watched the door to my room every night, wishing that it led anywhere but to the brothel. How trapped I'd felt.

I've felt trapped here, too, just in different ways.

We walk down to the kitchens together, and Ossev pauses on the threshold of the door that's magically locked. He runs a hand over it and the locks fall off, the heavy wood swinging open. A cold breeze immediately swirls inside, ruffling my hair and catching my skirts. I breathe it in and I'm filled with a heavy sense of relief.

Outside.

"Thank you," I say again.

"You're cold."

I shake my head. "It's fine." The cold feels good. It reminds me that we're high in the mountains at the edge of the world, but we are still a part of the world. Sometimes I feel all too disconnected when nothing but spiderwebs and stone walls surround me. "Will you come outside with me?"

Ossev nods, and I lead the way.

I step over the threshold and outside, crossing my arms over my chest at the bitter breeze. I need to make myself a thick cloak if I plan on going outside often. And if it's up to me, I will absolutely be going outside as frequently as possible. Pulling my fingers back into the warmth of my long sleeves, I tuck my hands under my arms and look around at the desolate landscape. I've been inside the tower so long I'd forgotten just how dreary and gray it is out here. The sky is overcast without a hint of sunlight peeping through, and the distant mountains enclose the nearby lake and the tower itself like a mouth with jagged teeth. I stare out at the lake. The surface is perfectly smooth, like glass, but I know that's deceiving. Out there are gigantic serpents that live under the surface.

I remember one swallowed Vitar whole. "Will the serpents hurt me? If I go near the water?"

"Nothing will hurt you," Ossev says. "We will not allow it."

For some reason, I find that answer pleasing. I know that my presence in the tower can be seen as imprisonment, but if they let me wander freely and without harm, it means I'm not so trapped as I thought. The realization helps a lot. I smile over at Ossev and then start walking, circling around the tower. It looks far more slender outside than it does on the inside, and I wonder if that is magic of some kind. Out here, it looks a bit like a lighthouse I saw on the coast once, tall and narrow, but the interior feels spacious and warm, if covered in webs. There's a long, chalky-looking cliff with stone stairs cut out of the rock, leading down to the shore. More stone stairs have been cut into the base of the tower, leading to a small grassy area that's overrun with knee-high weeds and scraggly ground cover.

"There used to be a garden here," says Ossev suddenly.

I turn to him in surprise. "Was there?"

He gazes out at the weedy surroundings. "Perhaps so. We have had visitors in the past that stayed for a long time. One might have made a garden."

"You can't recall? But your job is to view the past." I'm surprised he doesn't remember, because Ossev always seems so settled compared to Neska and Zaroun. Perhaps I've misinterpreted what his job truly is.

"I see the past," he agrees. "But I see so many that they run together after a while. I can search through my threads and look for mentions of a garden, but…" He shrugs. "It is unimportant. This area is yours now." His eyes glaze over and his expression grows distant. "Perhaps it was always your garden. Perhaps I am seeing a loop of time and not a thread."

I have no idea what that means, but I appreciate the gift nevertheless. "Thank you. I'm excited."

"Are you? Over a patch of dirt?"

"Over the freedom to work this patch of dirt, yes. To sit in the sun, should it ever come out, and to breathe in the fresh air." I smile up at him. "And to grow vegetables, if I can get them to grow at all. Having fresh food every now and then would be a lovely change."

Ossev gazes down at me. "You can go anywhere you like. I will leave the door in place for you. Just do not try to cross the Ashen Deep." He gestures out at the still waters. "Our boundary is there. Time flows differently once you leave our home, and one day might pass like two hundred years."

Oh. The feeling of being trapped returns again. "So those are your conditions?"

"If you want to leave, I will take you," he says, his gaze locked on mine. "But know that you will never be able to return if you do go. You cannot be an anchor if you leave."

I know this. Faith made it very clear when she was with Aron that she couldn't walk very far from him or it would pain her terribly. I imagine it would be the same—perhaps three times as awful—if I were to try and leave the tower of my own accord. But all the talk of leaving makes me think of something else. "Can *you* leave, Ossev?"

"I cannot."

His expression is blank, or perhaps he's hiding from me what he truly thinks about this fact. My captors are prisoners just as much as I am, and it soothes some of the resentment that I've had building. It's not that I wish to leave, of course. There's nothing out there for me to return to. But knowing that they're trapped just as much as I am makes things different.

There's an old Yshremi saying that a miserable sort always finds company. Perhaps that applies.

And yet…I don't truly feel miserable. A bit uncertain of my place, yes. I would like more to do, or just even more conversations. But I have all the fabric I could wish for, a belly full of food, and three masters that do not beat me or pass me around to strangers who will want more from me than I wish to give.

And now I have a garden.

And a door.

"Thank you, Ossev," I say in a soft voice. I reach out and touch his sleeve. "I love it. I hardly know where to begin to turn it into a garden, but I love it." I give him a flirty look, resorting back to my old tricks. "Are you trying to buy my affections, sir?"

"Is it working?" His expression is wistful. "The others get so much of you that I worry I will be forgotten. Zaroun has already won your heart. Neska is possessive and will monopolize you if he can."

"I am here for all three of you," I say, and lean in, pulling him down so I can kiss his cheek. "As for my affections, this is a wonderful start."

Ossev gazes down at me as if nothing else exists in the world. "Can I hold you while you sleep? Just to watch over you?"

Again, I'm surprised by his request. Here I'd thought I had Ossev figured out, and he continues to surprise me. "But your work…the strands. Don't you need to tend to them?"

He grins, looking the most human of the three aspects. "The

lovely thing about being in control of the past is that it is already done. There is no immediacy to my task."

I consider this. "Very well, then. I think I'd like some company in bed." I raise a finger at him. "But just holding. Nothing more."

"Holding is fine. I will take whatever you are comfortable with."

I slide my hand into the crook of his elbow and steer him back toward the tower. "It's not time to sleep just yet, but I don't mind company for a little longer."

Ossev remains at my side for most of the day, which surprises me all over again. I keep expecting him to disappear, and yet every time I turn around, he's right there, watching me as I tidy the kitchen and make myself food. He doesn't speak unless I ask him a question, and I get the impression that he's not used to holding conversations. I'm reminded of Neska's comment that they are connected in a way, and perhaps they have a mental link that doesn't require spoken dialogue. Whatever it is, he seems both uncomfortable and eager at my questions, and watches my every action.

I head up to Zaroun's quarters for my afternoon appointment, and as I do, Ossev melts into the shadows, disappearing away. When I leave Zaroun behind, hours later, he returns, his eyes bright. "Is it time for me to hold you?"

"I suppose it is," I tell him with a smile. I'm curious that I haven't seen Neska on this day. Is he avoiding the others? Do they all avoid one another? Or am I reading too much into things? "Come, then."

I lead Ossev into my chamber and ignore him as I ready myself for bed. I wrap my hair in the silk bonnet I've made to protect my curls, and take a bath, rubbing lotion into my skin to make it soft when I'm done. I change into the bright blue, simple nightgown I've made for myself out of the fabric here and climb into bed. The moment I pull the covers over myself, Ossev is there with me. He fits himself against my back under the blankets and wraps his arms around me, a little too tight to be comfortable.

Tapping his arm, I get him to ease off. "It's an affectionate caress, not the clutching of a toy about to be snatched away."

"Of course."

I relax in his arms, and can't help but notice that this is the first time one of them has shown interest in being with me while I sleep, like a partner would. I've never thought of any of them as partners, just beings I have to service. Perhaps we both need to look at each other differently. I consider this, and rub Ossev's arm. His skin is chilly, but he makes a sound of pleasure at my touch.

"Are you comfortable?" I ask him.

"I...do not know."

"You don't know?" I smile a little at that. "You're not sure?"

"I am not sure I understand 'comfort.' But I see others hold their wives in bed and they seem to get joy from it, so I wanted to try it."

I turn toward him. "And are you enjoying it?"

His answer is a very soft "Yes."

Smiling, I lean back against him. It's a bit like leaning against marble, but with a little adjusting, it's not uncomfortable. It's been a long time since I've shared my bed for sleeping. No one ever wants to just *sleep* with me. They always want something more.

It's that something more that keeps me awake for a while, because I know Ossev has other motives. Yet he's not pushing for anything more, just to hold me. I continue to think about Ossev, and a new idea occurs to me. "May I ask you something? Do you ever look at my threads?"

"I can, but not the others." His thumb lightly strokes my bare arm. "You're very soft."

But I'm fixated on his answer. "You can, but Zaroun and Neska cannot?"

He shakes his head. "The High God has hidden your fate from us so it does not drive us mad. If we saw your death, we could lose the balance we keep here. We would be so upset that everything would be affected." His breath is warm against my throat, and he rubs his face along the column of my neck. "I am not supposed to look either, but I cannot help a quick glance now and then."

Flattering. But also confusing. "Zaroun sees my death."

"No." When I stir in his arms, he explains. "He sees you dying. He sees all things dying. It is different. He sees every living creature speeding toward its natural end. It is difficult for him. He has the most difficult job of all, I think. It is why the High Father keeps us separated into our aspects. In other worlds, the God of Time was not so lucky and I suspect things went badly."

Poor Zaroun. I make a mental note that I will be extra kind and affectionate to him when I see him next. Not that this is a difficult task. Zaroun is sweet and wishes only to be given affection. To spend a few hours in my company. He never asks for anything more.

Ossev slides his arm around my waist and settles it there. "Is this...all right?"

I nod. It is because he asked. Ossev is trying, and to me, that's everything.

Ten

I wake up at some point, my skin prickling with awareness. Ossev's form is still pressed to mine, his arm around my waist. He's still, but I suspect he's not sleeping. I close my eyes again, but something keeps bothering me, and I open them once more, scanning the room.

Neska is in the doorway.

His gaze is locked upon the bed, where I'm curled with Ossev against me. I can feel the heat of emotion in the room. Neska's jealousy is palpable, and yet he says nothing.

Our eyes meet.

His mouth thins and then he walks away, disappearing down the corridor and I get the vague sense that I've done something wrong. Ossev did warn me that Neska was the most possessive, but my job is to serve all three of them, not just the one.

Is he jealous that the others are making progress with me? Would he rather that I treat the others with coldness while he gets all my affection?

Probably, now that I think about it. Annoyed at that realization, I tuck Ossev's arm closer against me and snuggle in against him, returning to sleep.

If Neska wants my body, he can take it at any time. If he wants my affection…he must earn it.

I'M NOT ENTIRELY SURPRISED THAT NESKA CATCHES ME when I'm alone later the next day. Ossev disappeared after I awoke, asking me for another quick kiss and then heading off to his work. I spent the morning with Zaroun, stroking his hair and telling him stories of the places I have been. Now that my time is my own, I want to eat a bite and then go and examine my garden. I want to see what I can make of the patch of land.

I should have known Neska would stop me.

"My lord," I say in an even voice. "I was just heading to the kitchens. Would you like to join me or do you have need of me elsewhere?"

His gaze is sharp as he regards me. "The kitchens will suffice."

I nod, trying to read his mood. He seems restless, but he could still be annoyed at the time I spent with his other selves—the other Aspects. "May I make you something? Tea? Food?"

"I do not eat. I do not drink." Yet he hovers behind me like a restless spirit as I walk down the long ramp that leads toward the kitchens.

Of course I know these things. I also know that Aron of the Cleaver, who I served before, would sometimes take food and drink on a whim, just to sample what the humans were tasting. Neska, I fear, is being obstinate. If he wishes to be stubborn, though, I will humor him. I ignore the god hovering at my heels as I craft a small plate of dried meat and fruits. I sit at the table and drink water, eating methodically and in silence.

All the while, I can feel Neska watching me.

Once I'm done, I pick up my dish and clean the small area of the kitchen I've used. I wanted to experiment with spicing and drying some more meat and some of the fruit from the cocoons, but that's messy, time-consuming work and I don't know that I want to do it with Neska observing me so intently. It's clear he wants something.

"Yulenna."

I pause. Is that the first time he's said my name? Addressed me as a person? It sends a pleasant shiver up my spine, because his tone is almost caressing. "Yes, my lord?"

His eyes are blazing as he regards me. "Get on the table."

It's a jarring request from Neska. *On* the table? Did I hear him correctly? I hesitate, and then the desire to please him takes over. I move to the table and consider it, my hand on the surface. The counter is tall, and so I'm not entirely surprised when Neska moves to my side and helps me up.

Then I'm perching atop the edge of the large wooden table in the center of the kitchen and wondering what it is he truly wants. Is he going to punish me in some way? It's impossible to tell from his expression. "Have I offended you, my lord?"

"I am not offended, no." He breathes deep, as if inhaling my scent, and then takes a step back. "Pull up your skirts for me."

Oh, is this sex? If so, I've misread his cues entirely. We haven't had sex in many days now—perhaps even weeks—ever since I told him how I truly felt. But perhaps he's grown tired of trying to consider my feelings and just wants relief. If so, I'm not surprised. It might be asking too much to demand a god humor my conflicted emotions. I tug my skirts up and shift my weight, exposing myself all the way to the waist. "Would you rather I bend over the table, my lord—"

"Hush," he tells me, a look of concentration on his face. "I am determined to get this right."

"Get what right?"

He gives me an annoyed look, as if I'm interrupting his focus. "On your back, Yulenna." Neska pauses briefly and then adds in a soft voice, "Please."

It's the "please" that tells me this is something different. I'm mystified, but I do as I am asked. I lie flat back on the table, staring up at the stone ceiling while Neska considers my bared body.

"I have seen a great many threads recently," he continues in a silky-soft voice. "Looking for a very specific sort of thing. I have watched a great many mortal men and women at work, and I have determined that the only way to truly understand this particular action is to learn it for myself." Neska's hand slides up my thigh, sending another shiver trembling through my body. "Has your cunt been licked before?"

I make a wordless sound in my throat, because of all the things I expected Neska to ask...this was not it. Neska, the most brooding, impossible, and selfish of the three...is going to pleasure *me*? "Yes it has."

"Excellent. Then you will tell me if I do something wrong."

That's the only warning I get before he moves fully between my thighs and kneels on the floor. A moment later, my legs are over his shoulders, and he presses his face against my pussy. I make another small sound in surprise. His skin is cool against mine and he gives my pussy a soft, gentle kiss...and then another. And another.

Soon, I'm being peppered with affectionate kisses. They feel good, and it's strange to realize that it's Neska being so tender, but I hope he doesn't expect me to climax from this. He did say he doesn't want me pretending. I want to run my hands through his hair like I do Zaroun, but I'm not sure if he'll like it. Neska in particular has never invited me to touch him.

His fingers drift over the seam of my pussy and then he spreads me open for his perusal. I quiver, waiting to feel his mouth on my skin.

"I watched so many threads," he murmurs. "And yet I find I still do not have the answers I sought." He strokes a finger up and down my slit, grazing through the wetness there. And then he pauses. "You're slick."

Inwardly, I tense, ashamed. I've had some men in bed that didn't like it when a woman had a bodily function, but I'm hoping that Neska's question is due to simple ignorance. "It's a natural reaction," I say in a quiet voice. "I cannot stop it."

"Is it? What are you reacting to?"

"When I'm aroused, I'll get wet."

He's quiet for a long moment. His finger strokes through my wetness again, and I tremble. "You have never been aroused with me before, have you?" His voice is cool, wondering.

I don't know if he's offended or not. "You've never tried to touch me before."

"Hm. This is true."

He doesn't seem to be offended, and I breathe a little easier.

"You're very tense," Neska points out. "Is this...unpleasant for you?"

I clench a hand in the dress pooled at my waist and try to think how to phrase my answer. "My desire to please you is warring with what I know from past encounters with men who did not want my reactions. Sometimes sex is messy, and some men do not like that. I am not certain what a god will think of a human body, and so yes, I'm tense."

"I am not a mortal. What they think does not concern me. Does this wetness...is it pleasing to you?" He lifts his hand and sniffs his fingers. "It smells unusual. Strong, but not distasteful."

"When I'm wet, I'm very pleased," I manage. "And when I'm touched with wet fingers, it feels better because everything glides."

"Hmm." He sounds more curious than anything. "When I come, is it wet like this?"

"Spiderwebs," I tell him. "It's spiderwebs."

Neska huffs, as if amused. "Interesting. Do you find it unpleasant?"

"It was unnerving at first, but I've gotten used to it."

He strokes his fingers up and down the cleft of my pussy, and I whimper.

"You make quite a lot of wetness," he declares. "I like that. I must arouse you very much."

Count on Neska to make it about himself. I'm amused at this particular observation and his smug response, but then he rubs a finger over the hood of my clit and I forget about everything. I suck in a breath, my body clenching, and he makes another pleased sound at my reaction.

"You're not pretending, are you?"

"If I was pretending, I wouldn't be wet."

"Hmm. You can't make yourself wet at will?"

I shake my head, and the answer pleases him. He fingers me again, gathering more wetness from the entrance of my body and stroking the bud of my clit with slick fingers. Even though my eyes are closed, I can feel him watching my expression closely. He's noting my responses, and adjusting his touches accordingly. He *wants* to learn, and I'm flattered.

As he casually fingers me, he adds, "Some used their mouths on their lovers."

Another whimper escapes me. "Some do, yes."

"What if I did such a thing? Would you like it?"

Is he volunteering? I squirm against his hand, panting. His other laying flat on the inside of my thigh and I'm aware of how close he's leaning, and how very wet I am...and how aroused. When he strokes his fingers through my folds again, my body makes a slick sound that just proves how turned on I am. He has to ask if I'd like his mouth on me? "Why don't you try it and find out?"

Neska isn't irritated at my sly comment. He huffs again, the sound one of amusement. "I do believe I shall."

And then he runs the tip of his tongue through my slick heat.

I moan, my legs jerking. My hands clench in my gown, and I'm desperate to hold onto something. When he makes a pleased sound at my taste, I decide to be bold and put a hand atop his head. I sink my fingers into his hair, and it's just as soft and silky as the others.

He stiffens at my touch, though, and I immediately jerk away. "I'm sorry," I blurt out. "I should have asked—"

"You want to touch me?" Neska's voice is low and it sounds astonished, as if he had no idea.

"It's natural to touch someone that's giving you pleasure." I try to keep my tone casual, even though my heart is racing. Is he offended? Annoyed? "I can stop if you don't like it."

"That is the first time you've reached for me, Yulenna."

Oh. So it is. The fact that he's calling me by my name feels momentous, too. Like we're making progress with something between us. "It's the first time I've wanted to."

"Then you may continue." He takes my hand in his and gently settles it back in his hair, and then pulls my wet folds apart and runs his tongue over them again, as if he was never interrupted.

I moan, my legs twitching again as he laps at me. I'm careful not to pull his hair, but it grows exceedingly difficult to pay attention as he tries out different ways of tonguing me to see what makes me respond.

"Your clit is just big enough that I can suck on it," he murmurs, breath warm against my skin. "I saw some women had very small ones, but I like yours. It fits against my tongue nicely."

And then he closes his lips over my clit and sucks, and I nearly come off the table. I cry out again when he clamps a hand down on my thigh, keeping me spread, and his mouth continues to work me over, sucking on my clit and then flicking at it with the tip of his tongue. I'm close to climaxing, and as he licks and toys with me, I arch against his mouth, unable to stay still. He keeps humming to himself, as if he has more to say but finds his mouth occupied, and the humming only adds to the sensation. When I come, it's with a ferocious clenching of my legs, a fresh gush of release, and the most wrenching, delicious orgasm I've had in years.

Perhaps ever.

I suck in deep breaths, dizzy. I'm vaguely aware of Neska peppering kisses on my pussy again, then the tip of his tongue gliding through my folds once more. I'm also aware that I have my hand clenched in his silky hair, tighter than is comfortable. With a gasp, I release him. "Oh. My apologies, my lord."

"No apology necessary. I liked that." He licks me again, and another tremor racks my body. When I open my eyes, I find him watching me from the seat of my thighs. "I found that excessively enjoyable. I shall have to do that more often."

"You...you will?"

"Indeed." He licks his lips and then slowly gets to his feet, while I stare at him from my wreckage atop the table. "Keep yourself bare for me, so I might have you at any time." He contemplates my sprawled legs and then reaches out, running a finger down my slippery cleft again, as if he can't resist. "Lovely. My other selves are going to be jealous that I had my tongue on you first, you know. They're going to want their turn."

They...are? I blink at him, dazed.

Neska regards me for a long moment, then swipes his thumb over his mouth. "Indeed." He considers my pussy, and then looks up at me again. "And since they will want their turn with you, I need to do it best. And the best way is to practice."

With that, he moves between my thighs again.

My hand goes back to his hair, and I'm stunned as he puts his mouth on me again. By all the gods in the Aether, is this going to be my new normal?

Neska strokes a finger into my wet channel and lowers his mouth to my clit, and then I forget everything, even how to breathe.

Eleven

Neska's discovery of oral sex leads to a strange sort of competition between the three Aspects. All of them are fascinated at suddenly making me come, and I find myself constantly accompanied by one of them, eager to make me climax.

It's as if they have a new toy, and the toy is me.

Neska makes me come at least four times that one afternoon, refusing to let me get off the table until I'm whimpering with fatigue. My limbs feel like jelly once he's done with me, and no sooner do I get to my quarters than Ossev is there.

"I want to try," is all he says, and then I'm flat on my back on my bed, with another Aspect's head between my thighs.

He wrings a rough, small orgasm from my body and then seems disappointed at my response. We have a conversation about how a mortal can only take so much before they're exhausted, so he curls up with me and holds me while I sleep.

Ossev is back between my legs when I wake, and this time he makes me come hard. Twice.

After that, Zaroun wants to pleasure me when I visit him instead of the other way around.

It's like everywhere I turn, I have a Spider god waiting to suck my clit until I scream. It's exhausting.

I...love it.

It's strange at first to have the tables turned upon me. I'm used to being the one that does the pleasuring, the one that must see to everyone else's relief. Rare is the lover that thought to do anything for me, and the fact that I have three of them at once, eager to go down on me at a moment's notice? That their satisfaction in licking my cunt comes from my satisfaction as much as theirs?

It's heady. I feel pampered and tired and very, very content with my lot.

For the next few weeks, the three Spidae are utterly focused on me and learning my body. They want to bathe me. They want to brush my hair for me and help me put on (or take off) my clothing. They want to touch every part of me and see my reaction to each touch.

And then come the gifts.

After Neska gifted me the mirror, and Ossev the garden, Zaroun has been asking me pointed questions, and I suspect he's been trying to think of a gift he can give me as well. There's a fierce competition between the three of them, which is baffling given that they're all Aspects of the same person. Yet they seem so different at times that if I hadn't met Aron of the Cleaver, I would think them triplets instead of Aspects.

Regardless, one cannot bestow upon me a kiss or a present (or an orgasm) without the others demanding equal attention. I know if I eat my midday meal with Zaroun, I will find either Ossev or Neska in the kitchens that evening, with the other waiting in my quarters.

I definitely feel like a favored toy being fought over.

Yet strangely enough, our boundaries remain. The Spidae are focused on pleasuring me, but no one asks me to service them in return. No one demands more than a kiss from me or for me to spread my legs. At first, it feels like a ploy—orgasms for me so I'll feel obligated to pleasure them in return—but Ossev explains to me that they truly enjoy touching me and getting my responses, and they do not want my touches unless I want to give them.

And I'm not sure if I'm ready to give them yet. So I hold off for a time. I'm happy to kiss and cuddle and let them go down on me, but I'm not ready to reciprocate just yet.

It's one night, while I'm in my bath with Zaroun, that he surprises me.

"How fares your garden?" he asks, holding me against his chest. My thick curls are wrapped in my silk bonnet and held out of the water, because it's not yet wash day and I'm too tired to fuss with cleaning and oiling my hair today. Zaroun doesn't mind, because he's also wearing something on his head—his blindfold. In this way, we're both comfortable in my tub, luxuriating in the warm water. I lie against his chest as he plays with my fingers, and we talk about everything and absolutely nothing at all.

"My garden hasn't started yet," I confess to him. Between constantly being called away for pleasuring, I haven't had the time or strength to truly get to work on it. "I've cleared some of the beds but I've gotten no further just yet."

"Apple?" he asks. "What about apple?"

I frown down at our joined hands. "You like apples?"

"I see apple."

Most of the time Zaroun's comments have to be deciphered, and so I don't find this too alarming. "Apples come from trees, and I don't know that we can make an apple tree work." I run a soapy hand up his arm. "You see apples though?"

"Smiling. Happy."

Well, that could be me, or that could be anything. "I'm happy right now," I confess, and strangely enough, it's the truth. My last lover prior to arriving here—Solat, who travels with Aron of the Cleaver and his anchor—was handsome enough, if not the most generous of lovers. And traveling with Aron allowed me to escape the brothels that seem to be the end-point of most attractive female slaves. True, there isn't anyone around to talk to except the Spidae themselves, and the weather is bleak and dreary every day, and if I want food or a particular piece of clothing I must craft it myself…and yet, I am happy. My belly is full. I have a home to call my own and I am not being forced to service anyone with my body. I'm the one being serviced. I know I'm supposed to be helping the Spidae by being their anchor, but this last week, I feel as if I've been getting more out of things than they have.

That might be all the orgasms speaking, though.

But yes, I am happy. It's not anything I would have imagined for myself, but I'm content and even looking forward to what each day brings.

I don't think anything of our conversation until the next day, when one of the spiders approaches me in the kitchen and drops an apple at my feet.

That makes me pause, blinking.

I've grown used to the spiders that move about the tower, silently creeping in the webs that cover every surface. While I thought they were unnerving at first, now they're just more of the tower's fixtures, just like the gods themselves. The spiders appear occasionally to bring me bundles of food wrapped in webbing, too. Sometimes it's fruit and nuts scavenged from who only knows where, and sometimes it's a freshly killed animal. That took a little more getting used to, but I've learned to be more comfortable with it, knowing that the Spidae are directing the spiders to bring me such things.

They all want me strong and healthy, and so I've learned to overlook my squeamishness to enjoy the variety of things they bring me to prepare.

So I pick up the apple and smile at the spider in my kitchens. "For me?"

It crouches low, its hindquarters in the air, and gives a little wiggle. I'm reminded of a puppy, and while the face and legs are certainly not dog-like, there's a sweet, innocent air to the spider. He looks as if he just wants to please me.

I beam at him and shine the apple on my dress. "Thank you very much. I love apples."

The spider trots away and I return to tying bundles of herbs to dry.

A moment later, another apple rolls to my feet. When I look up, the spider gives another wiggle of delight, and I can't help but laugh.

Well...I did say I liked apples.

Twelve

Over the next three days, the spider continues to show up over and over again, bringing me more and more apples. It makes me smile each time, and I start to look forward to my new friend visiting me. He always waits in the kitchens, and I've taken to saving scraps to feed him. Spiders still aren't cute or cuddly, and one the size of a pony is definitely not either of those things...but he's growing on me.

I start calling him Apple, and it seems I have a pet.

Apple follows me outdoors into the gardens as I dig at the rocky soil, and I drop fruit-cores and potato ends with roots growing out of them into the dirt and add composted kitchen scraps to the heap. It doesn't look promising, as everything here is gray and cold. I'm determined to grow something, but my seedlings don't look hardy enough to survive the weather here.

I glance over at the enormous spider. The apples it brings me are always fresh and juicy. "Where are you getting your fruit, love?"

It trills and wiggles its hind end, scampering away a step and then returning. Apple clearly wants to play. I pick up a nearby stick, unsure if it's going to appease the spider, but when he (I think Apple shall be a he until I learn otherwise) races off to chase it, I suppose some games are universal. We play with the stick, me tossing it ahead of myself and Apple rushing to fetch it as I circle around the tower that afternoon. I make sure to stay far away from the water's edge and as I gaze out on the gray, bleak lands and the jagged mountain peaks, I see no animal life. There are no birds, no rabbits, no foxes, nothing that might hint at life.

There's only me and Apple…and the tower.

When we return inside, Apple is shivering and moves toward the small fire I keep going inside the hearth. I stoke the coals as I heat my dinner and ponder this strangeness. If Apple is cold outside of the tower, how are he and his brothers able to go about and retrieve food for me? Every day there are fresh pods of fruit or vegetables or meat. Given how barren it is outside, they must be traveling long distances to bring me such things…aren't they?

Once I'm done eating and clean my dishes, Apple races away from the kitchen, heading up the winding ramp into the heart of the tower. I call out after him, amused. "Did you hear something?"

There's no response, so I pick up my skirts and head up, since the Spidae haven't called for me. I might as well do a bit of sewing. I'm working on a lovely blue dress with ridiculous, floor-length sleeves made entirely of exquisitely tiny, golden fabric pleats, mostly to see if I can. I'm eager to get it done and wear it, just for the simple pleasure of dressing myself in a frothy concoction.

When I get to my room, though, Zaroun is standing in the midst of my things, the blindfold on his face and his head tilted toward the ceiling. "Oh," I say by way of greeting. "Have you been waiting for me long, my lord? I was following one of the spiders."

Apple is nowhere to be seen, though. He's probably making himself scarce now that one of the masters is here.

Zaroun tilts his head towards me and a smile curves his delicate mouth. "He is a good friend to you."

Is this the future he is seeing, or a general comment? I can never tell with Zaroun. I decide it doesn't matter, because if Apple is in my life for a long time, I think that would be a good thing.

I've never had a pet, and though the spider is unconventional, his sweet nature and playfulness makes me laugh. "So far he has been, yes." I move to his side and touch his arm, my instinct to please him rising. "What can I assist you with, my lord? I am here to serve."

Zaroun reaches up and brushes his fingers over my jaw, then dips his head toward mine. His lips whisper over my mouth, sending a prickle of hunger through my body. "It has been too long since I tasted you."

A curl of delight unfurls in my belly. "It has been less than a day, Zaroun."

"Far too long," he agrees. "My mouth is parched and only your taste will slake my thirst." He kisses me again, this time lingering. Zaroun doesn't kiss with the desperate need of Ossev or the intense conquest of Neska. His kisses are always light and fluttery, a tease and a promise more than ownership. I like all the kisses for their uniqueness, but Zaroun's kisses make me feel treasured. Special.

I'm breathless as he kisses my upper lip and then begins to press his mouth along my jaw. My arm curls around his neck and I hold him close as his mouth tickles my earlobe. "Where do you want me, my lord? On the bed?"

"I want you open to my mouth. I want you hot and wet and clenching around my tongue. I do not care where." And he nips my ear.

Shivering with arousal, I tug him towards my bed. I've noticed that Ossev and Neska will take their turns with me anywhere and everywhere—in the hall, in the kitchen, against a wall, bent over my bathtub—but Zaroun always asks where I prefer. He's definitely the sweetest and most thoughtful of the three. I sit on the edge of the bed and he kisses down my throat, his hands moving to my breasts. They're trapped in the tight boning of my corset, but he plumps them with his hands, pressing against the sides of my gown before kissing the rounded mound of each one. Then he moves lower, to where my thick petticoats cover my legs.

Before I can reach down, he flips them up and then sighs with satisfaction when he breathes in my scent. "I do like the smell of you, my lovely anchor. You always smell mouth-watering."

"Do I?" I ask, breathless.

"Today you smell like outdoors, too." He leans in and inhales deeply between my thighs, and I squirm. I try not to find anything unusual with what they do in bed, reminding myself that they are gods and perhaps gods are into different things than most mortal men. Things like flipping a woman's skirts up and just drinking in her scent and doing nothing else for long, shiver-inducing moments. He nuzzles my mound and drags his open mouth over the insides of my thighs, making sounds of satisfaction as he does. "So sweet."

I try to stay still, even though I want to squirm and lift my hips up against his mouth. "I should take my shoes off. I was wearing them in the garden..."

"Lovely, lush garden," he agrees.

Oh...is it lovely and lush in the future? Then things do grow here?

"But I am not interested in your shoes," Zaroun continues. "Just your cunt."

And then he licks me.

I gasp, the breath shuddering out of me at the feel of his hot, slick mouth on my sensitive skin. Instinctively, my hands go to his head and I hold him in place as he licks between the cradle of my thighs, teasing and tasting. His tongue toys with my clit, making me whimper, and his fingers play along my folds. It's like he's touching me everywhere, and when his mouth goes from light and playful to intense and focused, my orgasm builds. I'm moaning and clutching him as he works my pussy, driving me relentlessly toward climax.

When I come, it's with shattering intensity. I cry out as I come, utterly wrecked. Satiated, panting, I flop back against the blankets to catch my breath. "Oh, my. That was lovely."

"Not done," he murmurs, his teeth grazing one of my now-sensitive folds. "I need more."

I whimper, but I'm helpless to obey. I know how this works with them. They fixate on pleasuring me (though I suspect they get a great deal of satisfaction with it, too) and I might be held down for at least five or six orgasms before Zaroun is done with me.

My legs twitch at the thought, and then Zaroun taps my thigh. "You are moving too much."

"Sensitive," I pant, trying to be still and failing. "Very sensitive."

"You should sit on my face again," he says. "I liked that very much."

I go still. "Again...?"

"Have we not done that yet?" He presses kisses to my pussy, sending quivers through my body. "I have seen it quite clearly." Zaroun pauses, and then drags his tongue slowly and achingly over my clit, causing me to emit the most needy mewling sound ever. "Mmm, yes, I have definitely heard that before. Come. I want more sounds from you and less thrashing."

Am I thrashing too much? I whimper, but when he gets on the bed, adjusting his blindfold and then reaching for me, I'm helpless to protest. Part of me is exhausted, but a larger part of me wants to sit on his pink, flushed mouth and his pale, aquiline nose. Part of me wants to bear down on his perfect face and grind against him and if that's not the most delicious mental image, I don't know what is.

Gathering my skirts, I straddle his face with trembling thighs, and he pulls me down against his mouth. His tongue seeks out the entrance to my body and then he's pushing into me with wet, lapping thrusts. I moan, clutching at the headboard of the bed, and throw my head back. I'm riding a god's face...at his bequest. And something tells me that from the pleased noises he's making, he's not going to let me up anytime soon.

This new position has me facing the door to my room,

though, and when my eyes flutter open, I realize someone is standing in the doorway.

It's Neska, watching me ride Zaroun's face.

I gasp, startled. My pussy clenches as Zaroun thrusts his tongue deep again, his groan one of delight. I stare at Neska, wondering how my possessive Spidae will take the sight of me being tongued by one of the other Aspects. His eyes narrow as he watches me, and when I can't help but grind down against Zaroun's face, a hint of a flush moves over his pale cheeks.

He's not saying anything.

He's not leaving, either.

I rock against Zaroun's talented mouth, and even as I do, I reach out for Neska. It's an invitation, but it's also me just wanting to touch him as much as I'm being touched. To show him that there's no need to be jealous. That I can handle more than one lover at once. That I'm here to serve all three of the Aspects.

His silver gaze focuses on my outstretched hand. For a moment, I think he'll refuse my silent request, but then he sweeps into my chamber, coming to stand at the head of the bed and on the other side of the headboard that faces the door.

"Is he doing a good job?" Neska asks, his tone remote and detached as he studies my face.

I open my mouth to reply, only for Zaroun to lash his tongue inside me again, and I hunch forward, whimpering with pleasure even as I rock against him. My clit brushes against his nose, and it's the most exquisite torture.

"He doesn't have to breathe, you know," Neska murmurs, putting a finger under my chin to force me to look in his eyes. "He can stay under your skirts all day, smothered by your sweet, wet cunt."

I moan, my lashes fluttering at the mental image. I clutch the headboard harder, wishing I was naked so Neska could put his hands on my breasts. So he could touch me everywhere. I envision all three of them touching me at once, swarming over me in a tangle of bodies, and the idea takes my breath away.

I suddenly want that more than anything.

"You do, do you? Interesting." Neska's voice remains detached, though his eyes are full of silver fire. "You are a hungry little anchor, aren't you? You just need to be touched the right way." He brushes his thumb over my lower lip. "You need to be wanted and appreciated for who you are. And you need to be pleasured." He traces my mouth. "Between the three of us, I think we should never let you out of bed."

The thought makes me moan again.

"You like that, too," Neska all but purrs. "Sometimes it makes me wonder if you are serving us, or if it is we who are serving you." His thumb dips into my mouth, pushing down on my lower lip.

I capture it and suck on it hard, a promise in my eyes.

His gaze flares with heat, and he feeds a finger into my mouth. When I take it, panting, our gazes locked, he adds a second, and then a third. It's like he's trying to push my boundaries, but he needs to realize that nothing is forbidden, nothing is off limits when all parties want it equally. And for the first time, I realize I no longer hold resentment for them for my service. They no longer see me as just a plaything to be used. They like touching me and pleasing me as much as I like pleasing them.

Neska slowly pumps his three fingers in and out of my mouth, working them slickly even as I roll my hips against Zaroun's tongue. I've been so focused on Neska that I didn't realize how close I was to the edge. I'm coming suddenly and my hands fly to Neska's wrist, holding him in place as I whimper through my climax, shuddering and sucking hard on his fingers while stars bloom behind my eyelids and a haze of pleasure rolls through my body like the tide.

By the time I'm myself again, I feel wrung out and sated, but like something is still missing. I suck on Neska's fingers and then pull them from my mouth, letting his wet fingertips trail over my lips. "How can I serve you my lord?" I whisper. "Because I am here to serve."

His throat works, and for a moment, he gazes at me with such yearning and need that it takes my breath away. "Would you... touch me? Of your own need? Not of mine?"

How do I refuse that? How does anyone with a heart refuse such a request, especially when it's filled with such aching need?

So I nod and tug on his hand. I pull him toward the bed, indicating he should join us, but he looks at the bed and then thinks for a moment.

Zaroun nods to an unspoken command and squeezes my flank. "Hold on."

Hold on?

It's the only warning I get before Zaroun slides forward, and then I'm on the edge of the mattress. The headboard is suddenly gone and Neska is standing there, stroking my hair back from my damp brow and gazing at me with that hungry lust on his face. I'm still straddling Zaroun's face, his seeking tongue burying itself inside me again, and I gasp. "The—the headboard...?"

"I will return it when we are done," Neska says, running his thumb over my lower lip again. "Unless you do not want me here...?"

I shake my head, trying to focus my mortal brain around such things. Just as Ossev gave me a door, I guess Neska can get rid of half of my bed. I clutch at his hips as Zaroun mouths me with abandon, my oversensitive pussy quivering with every stroke of his seeking tongue. Neska stands still in front of me, just caressing my face, and I get the impression that he's waiting to see what I do.

He wants me to reach for *him*. He wants me to give him what I *want* to give him.

It feels like such a heady reversal of our early relationship that for the first time in my life, I feel powerful and in control. I run my hand over his clothed chest and gaze up at him, at the eyes that are narrowed and hungry, as if he's afraid to hope for too much. "I want you naked, my lord."

The moment I speak the words, his robe disappears under my hand. My fingers touch hard, muscled torso, pale and lean. His build is spare, just like the others, tall and lithe and somehow otherworldly. He's pale, too, but perfectly made, and I stroke my hand down that marble-like abdomen to his groin. Even here, he's flawless. There's not a pore to be seen, nor a blemish. His cock juts out, long and slender and perfectly made, with a delicate vein tracing over the length of his shaft.

Zaroun shifts his face, sucking on my clit, and I whimper even as I reach for Neska's perfect cock.

I caress him, stroking my hand up and down the length of him and learning his feel. Even his sac is gorgeous—which feels strange to say, as it's one of the ugliest parts of a male body on a normal man. On a mortal man, balls are wrinkled and saggy and covered in coarse hairs, but Neska is as perfect as Zaroun, his sac two perfect, plump globes encased in porcelain skin without a hint of a wrinkle or a hair. It should be downright unnatural, but it just looks like everything else with these gods—utter perfection and slightly otherworldly.

A bead pearls on the tip of Neska's cock, turning to a strand of webbing as it drips down from the head towards the blankets. I brush the pre-cum off of the head, watching as it's immediately replaced. There's a slight hint of a flush to his skin, and I lean forward to kiss the tip of his cock.

He immediately jerks in my grip, just as Zaroun tongues deep into my pussy again.

I gasp, clinging to Neska's cock, my other hand on his hard thigh for balance. "Can I touch you how I like?" I ask Neska, breathless. The question seems like a silly one, because I can't think straight, can't stop myself from rubbing his perfect length against my face, my lips. I can't help but run my hand over his skin, over the turgid shaft that practically throbs with need when I wrap my fingers around him.

"However you like," he says, and for once, he sounds as breathless as me. "Take your pleasure."

I moan at his wording, because sucking a cock is normally not about *my* pleasure at all. But with Zaroun sending quiver after quiver into my pussy as he lavishes attention to my core, I can't help but be aroused at the thought of making Neska come. Of taking him in my mouth and working him even as I ride his other Aspect's face. It feels decadent and yet so very right.

Gripping the base of his shaft, I lean forward and feed the head of him between my lips, keeping them pursed to add friction as I push him against my tongue. His breath stutters, and Zaroun moans even as he moves back to my clit, lavishing it with attention. I whimper, forgetting to be delicate with Neska and to take my time.

"It's all right," Neska whispers, caressing my cheek as I mouth him. "Take what you need."

Moaning, hungry to make him come, I suck him deep. I've had a lot of practice with pleasuring men with my mouth, and so it's easy for me to relax my jaw and push forward until he's deep, the head of him being constricted by my throat. I love the stutter of his breath, and I let my mouth flood with saliva to lubricate things even as I slowly move my head to pump him, hollowing my cheeks and breathing through my nose. It requires concentration and practice, and I'm so focused on sucking him that I've almost forgotten about Zaroun between my thighs until he sucks on my clit, hard—

—and then another orgasm tears through me, sharp and bright.

I'm so startled that I involuntarily gasp, and in doing so, suck Neska deeper. It's too much. When Neska groans, I pull back, coughing for air even as he floods my mouth with his release. The webs drip from my lips, strands between my face and Neska's cock, and Zaroun makes another sound of contentment, as if he's happy that we've both come at once.

Reaching out to Neska, I stroke his thigh and lick the webbing off his cock. "I'm sorry, my lord. That wasn't nearly as long as it should have been. I'll do better next time."

"You were distracted." His voice is still arrogant and aristocratic, but there's a faint thread of amusement in his tone. He strokes my cheek again, long, spidery fingers curling around my chin. "I will allow it. Did you...enjoy yourself?"

"Too much," I admit, and he gives me a rare smile.

I smile back and it feels...good. Natural. Easy.

Thirteen

After that, Neska leaves to return to his threads. Zaroun insists on bathing me, and so we climb into the tub together, him leisurely pouring handfuls of water over my skin as I relax against his chest. I'm boneless and exhausted, but in the best kind of way.

My head is full of churning thoughts in contrast to my sated body. I think about Neska, and how he'd watched us, and Zaroun hadn't noticed or cared. I think about how when I touched Neska, Zaroun would moan in pleasure. Do they all watch each other take turns with me? Do they all three feel it when I touch one of them? Or are they so connected in each other's heads that they feel another's response and react? If so, why be jealous of each other? There must be more to it.

"There is," Zaroun murmurs lazily, tracing wet circles on my breast. "But it is not for a mortal to understand."

I turn to look at him, because I know I didn't say such things aloud. "Are you prying into my mind?"

He just smiles, his eyes covered by the now-wrinkled blindfold. "Perhaps you are just easy to read?"

Hmm. I don't know if I believe that. I've always been good at hiding my emotions. It's part of the job.

A spider scuttles into the room and drops a pod near the door just as my stomach growls. A wry laugh escapes me, because of course the Aspect of the Future would know when I'm going to be hungry. The sight of the spider reminds me of earlier, though, and Apple. "Is that more fruit?" I ask him. "How do the spiders find it and bring it here when there's nothing growing around the tower?"

"They follow the threads."

Another enigmatic answer. "What threads?"

"The *threads*." He teases wet fingers around my nipple, making it tighten. "They stretch from life to life, but also from plane to plane and place to place. There is nowhere and no-when that cannot be accessed. The spiders see our needs and seek them out for us."

Hmm. "Do you think they could bring me a recipe book? Or sweets? Something other than just fruit?"

"Again?"

Again, huh? "Yes, again." I smile as he nuzzles my throat. "What can I say? I desire sweet things."

"Then you should always have what you desire." And his hand trails under the water to between my thighs, and then I'm not thinking about sweets (or anything) for hours.

"And that is how I acquired a pet spider," I tell Aron's anchor through my mirror. "I think they have told him to watch me and get things that I need, but I like the company."

"A pet spider named Apple," Faith echoes, blinking at me through the mirror. "You...you know that's not normal, right? You know that's fucked up?"

I chuckle, because Faith has such a crass way of saying things, and yet I appreciate her bluntness. "I know. But I like Apple. He's very sweet and eager to please." I push the needle through the soft, gauzy material I'm working on, glancing down at my embroidery work. "And the fact that he's a spider doesn't bother me any longer. I was wary of them when I first arrived, but I've grown used to the sight of them hiding in corners and lurking on the walls."

In the mirror, Faith shudders delicately. "I am appalled. I mean, if you want a puppy, ask for a puppy."

I tie off my stitches and lean in to bite the thread now that I've finished my work. "I'd be afraid Apple would eat the puppy."

"This is an absolutely horrifying conversation," Faith tells me in a cheerful voice. "Holy shit, and I thought things were weird here in Aron's realm with all the sparks and lightning storms and people trying to fight each other at a moment's notice. But you win. You are officially the anchor with the worst job. I won't even fight you for the title."

Am I the anchor with the worst job? "I truly think you are overstating things."

"Me? Be dramatic? Never." Faith grins at me through the mirror. "I'm glad you called, though."

"Called?"

She waves a hand, dismissing my confusion. "Figure of speech from my world. I'm just thrilled to hear from you. You...you're good, right? You're happy? You don't feel like we abandoned you?"

Her seeking gaze in the mirror is worried. I'm touched that she's so concerned. I truly didn't know what to think of the three Spidae and my choice to remain here when I initially made the decision. It felt as if I were out of options and only one true path to take. Yet as time passes and we all settle in with each other, I find that my contentment grows by the day. I look forward to seeing Zaroun, Neska and Ossev when they stop me in the halls or wake me from my sleep. I'm no longer worried that something is wrong when they approach me. I have fine dresses and all the food I can eat. I have a garden. I have a pet. I have endless, endless orgasms and three lovers who want nothing more than to make sure I'm well-pleasured, even though I'm supposed to be serving them.

"Quite happy...I know it is not what you would choose but I like it here and the Spidae are very kind to me."

"Oh yeah, because I see them and think, 'Now those are three very kind bros,'" Faith scoffs.

Eyeing my needlework, I pick up a new color of silk thread and thread the needle. "You may not believe me, but they are. Perhaps they are not caring to everyone, but they are generous with me." I pause, my face growing hot because I think of yesterday and how I rode Zaroun's face while I suckled on Neska. "Very generous."

"Mmm."

I clear my throat. "And you? How fares Aron? How fares your bond?"

Faith launches into a long story, telling me about everything that's happened since they left the tower (and me) behind. Aron has returned to his home plane, and brought Faith with him to the Plane of Storms. I did not realize such a thing was possible, but it makes sense. I saw how he watched Faith. He would never leave her behind.

It was one reason why I knew I needed to find a new place, a new master to serve. No one wants the old bed slave loitering when they are with the woman they love. Faith is kind and open-minded about such things, but I felt uncomfortable. No one wants to overstay their welcome with a moody god, and Aron was far more volatile than the three Spidae.

Thinking about my new masters makes me smile. I listen to Faith's story as she speaks, but part of my focus is on my masters. Neska's mirror allows me to speak to Faith as well as granting me the ability to watch whatever and whomever I should choose. I like that freedom, but I haven't had much of a chance to utilize it just yet. I've been more or less with one of the Spidae at all times recently, and I fully expect to see at least one of them the moment our conversation is done. They're going to want attention, I suspect, which will mean I'll probably end up on my back with someone's head between my thighs...

...or straddling another face. The thought makes my pussy clench with arousal. You would think with all of the attention I've been getting, it would make me want a reprieve, but it's just making me crave their touches even more. My fingers tremble, making it difficult to thread the needle. I can't stop thinking about last night with Neska and Zaroun. How even though there were two of them, it still felt as if it was all about me and my pleasure. After my bath, I'd been alone with my thoughts, and I haven't seen any of them today.

Things keep progressing with us. The next time I see one of them, am I going to pounce and demand that we fuck again, but this time I need to come too? Who will approach me first, I wonder. I haven't seen Ossev since early yesterday, and I fret that he's perhaps jealous that he wasn't included. Neska is usually the jealous one and Ossev far more mild and easy-going, but how will he handle both of the other Aspects getting in bed with me at the same time and not him?

"And so I said to Aron, you know what the Plane of Storms needs? Ducks. Lots of ducks."

"Mmm." I push the needle into the fabric in my hands, trying not to worry. This particular sash I'm embroidering is for Neska. I've made one for Zaroun—a night sky full of stars on a deep blue sash. Neska's will be the brightest part of day, with a bold sun against a vivid blue sky. I haven't yet decided what Ossev's will be, though.

"And at least one Canada goose, just to mess with everyone else. Though I don't know if you call them Canada geese here, seeing as you don't have Canada. But if you want a duck that will fuck your shit up, that's the one. Am I right?"

"Absolutely," I murmur. Purples and pale orange for Ossev, I think. That would be lovely. All the colors of dawn against a beige sash. I like that idea.

"Yulenna! You aren't even listening to me!"

I look up from my project, startled at the indignant sound of my name. "W-what?"

Faith shakes her head at me, but there's a smile on her face. "You're off in la-la land daydreaming. I just told you Aron needed ducks."

"What are ducks?" I ask, baffled, and put my sewing aside.

"Exactly!"

"I apologize. You're right that I'm distracted. I'm just thinking about...things." And I smile.

Faith puts a hand up to the mirror. "I'm going to stop you right there, because the last thing I want are sexy details about the spider guys. If you'd rather, we can talk tomorrow instead." She eyes her mirror, lowering her hand. "We can talk every day on this thing, right?"

"I believe so?"

"Then I'll talk to you tomorrow. Go kiss your boyfriend. Or boyfriends. Or watch them kiss. I don't care. I'll talk to you tomorrow." She waves at me, winks, and then the mirror goes dark.

Watch them kiss? I'm amused and intrigued, but I doubt it'll happen. Getting two of them in the room at the same time is all but impossible...and I'm not entirely sure they would like it anyhow. Perhaps it would be a bit too much like touching themselves given that their thoughts are connected.

A hand touches my shoulder and someone bends over me to press a kiss to my neck. "You are smiling. I like seeing that."

Oddly enough, I can tell by the inflection—and the kiss—that it's Ossev. I lean into his touch. "I was wondering if you were avoiding me."

"Never. Why would I?"

Should I say something? Or should I let one of the others? Or does he already know? I hesitate, uncertain, and decide to steer the conversation (and my thoughts) in a different direction. "You haven't been to see me today."

"Have I not? Time can be such a fickle thing. You know we

pay no attention to such things here." He presses another kiss to my throat, and his soft as spiderwebs hair falls over my shoulder. "I have been lost in my work."

Mmm. If it was distracted Zaroun or even controlling Neska, I might believe that a bit more. Ossev seems the most separated from his task, though, and I suspect it has something to do with the nature of it. He can put his work aside far more easily than the others. But Ossev saying he was lost in the webs? I don't entirely buy it. "If you're certain that's all it was..."

He hesitates, lifting his head, and I know I am right. I know there is something else bothering him.

"What is it?" I ask softly, turning in his arms to face him. "You can tell me."

Ossev's expression changes to a sly one. "I have been breaking the rules again."

Breaking the rules...? "Oh?"

"I am watching you from my threads. I am 'cheating.' The High Father would think me naughty." The look on his face is anything but contrite, though. He seems rather smugly pleased with himself, and at the same time, he cannot take his eyes off of me. His gaze turns hungry, devouring, and my body tingles with awareness as he studies me.

Oh, I know just what this naughty god has been doing. Feigning innocence, I ask, "And what is it you watched?"

"You. With the others."

He doesn't seem upset about it. Here I'd been worried that he'd feel neglected. "And what did you think?"

"I liked it." Ossev's blue eyes gleam with intensity. "I liked watching you be touched. I liked seeing hands on you and a cock in your mouth."

I bite back a gasp, as this is the most forward Ossev has been. It seems he likes being a voyeur. "And you weren't jealous?"

"Should I be?" He toys with my sleeve, then teases a fingertip under the thick fabric of my collar and brushing it against my bare skin. "Their hands are my hands, even when I am not there. I see them touching you and it is easy to envision myself in their place. To think it is myself being touched like that. To imagine it is my cock between your soft lips."

I move closer to him, putting my hand on his chest. His words are full of intensity and hunger, but not jealousy. I'm glad. I stroke my fingers down his front, smiling. "I would have liked you there."

"Next time I will be. You can sit on my face. I care naught, as long as I get to touch you. As long as I get to participate in your pleasure and watch you come, I am content."

"You just like watching," I purr at him, amused.

"I like watching *you*," he corrects. "It is different with you. I have seen a hundred thousand human threads and find none as interesting as yours, because you belong to us. Because you are here for us, and you are ours to please. It's different."

I wonder briefly if he would feel the same way with any anchor. Perhaps not. Would another anchor stand up to their demands and insist on not being used like a thing without feelings? Or would they say nothing and only interact with the Spidae when release was needed? Would that even help them touch their humanity? Or would it make them sink further into their aloofness?

Is it arrogant to think they might need...me?

"Not arrogant," Ossev rasps, his arm sliding around my waist. "You are good at making us see you. You are not just a body. You are Yulenna, who loves pretty dresses even when there's no one to see them. You are our woman, who gardens and hums when she sews. You are a person that loves to bathe, that laughs when she tells stories, and one that cannot bake bread no matter how hard she tries."

I giggle at that. "I should be mad that you're sneaking into my thoughts."

"But you are not."

I am not, no. I'm starting to expect it. And in a way, it's not a bad thing. They can sense my mood and my anger without me having to speak it. We will never be false with each other again. The Spidae will know if they're not pleasuring me in bed and how I feel about such things…and now they know me well enough to *care*.

"And are you here to make me come?" I ask lightly, tracing a finger around Ossev's nipple through his filmy robes. "To let me ride your face?"

"Yes," he rasps, his gaze full of intensity. "I would like that very much."

A new idea strikes me and I continue to tease his nipple. "Want to have sex?"

"I just said I did."

"No, Ossev. Read my thoughts. I want you inside me. Like we were before. But this time, we both want it."

To my surprise, he flinches and the look in his eyes changes.

Oh. I've hurt him. I don't need to be a mind-reading god to know that. "Ossev, I didn't mean that—"

"You did," he says, shaking his head. He takes my hand in his and turns it over, pressing a kiss to my palm. "But I understand now what you mean when you say that. I did not before. I did not care. But now that I know you, I know what the difference is between a Yulenna that endures my touch, and a Yulenna that embraces it." His mouth moves against my skin in soft, feathery kisses as he lavishes attention on my palm, and then moves to kiss the tip of each finger, his gaze on me. "Now that we know the difference, I wish we could go back and fix the past and how we were to you before. I have looked into it, but we are to guide the threads for others, not ourselves. I have no power over that."

I'm touched that he even tried. That he cares enough to want to change the experiences in the past. They were not bad experiences, just emotionless ones. I've certainly had worse.

"Just because you have had worse does not make them right," Ossev murmurs, kissing the tip of my thumb. "One greater wrong does not excuse lesser wrongs."

"You are a god," I tell him, flustered. "You do not need to apologize to anyone."

"Not even to you?"

My heart squeezes. "I...we're still figuring each other out, Ossev. All four of us. I am here to bring you in touch with your humanity, yes? To remind you what it is to be human so you can better serve those you look after. I wouldn't be here if you did not need such reminders. You wouldn't *need* me. If we get things wrong at first, that is the *most* human of problems."

I chuckle, but he doesn't join me, and my heart squeezes all over again because he looks miserable. Of the three, Ossev might be the most sensitive, the most in touch with his feelings. He will be my best friend of the three, I realize, and it makes me care for him all the more.

Reaching up, I caress his cool cheek and smile at him. "You listened to my complaints when I protested, and even though you could have bent me to your will and twisted me as easily as you twist the strands, you did not. You listened, and you made efforts to please me. That is all anyone could ever ask for, Ossev. There's no need to rewrite history when we can learn from it."

He gazes down at me, his blue eyes bright and aching. "We could ask for kisses. You said we could not ask for more, but I will always ask for kisses."

I laugh. "Every time you ask, I will be happy to give."

"Then I am asking right now."

Still chuckling, I put my other hand on his cheek and tilt my face up, moving in to kiss him. Our lips meet and he wraps his arms around me, his embrace achingly sweet. He holds me as if I'm the most precious thing in the world to him, his lips on mine. We kiss for a long time, nipping and caressing and teasing with tongues, until I'm aching with the need for more. I continue to kiss him, my tongue gliding deeper into his mouth in a suggestive manner. "Come to the bed."

Ossev groans, nodding. To my surprise, though, he doesn't push me down on the mattress or take the lead. He just gazes at me, those blue eyes bright with heat, and waits. He's letting me lead.

So I take his hand and guide him over to the bed. I sit him on the edge of it and undress him with careful touches, skimming my fingers over his pale, perfect flesh. When he's naked, we kiss again, and then he helps me undress, his expertise with threads obvious as he unties the laces on my corset with speed. My dress falls to the floor and I step out of it, settling onto his lap. His arms go around me, and he gazes up at my face, waiting.

Waiting for me to tell him what I want in bed. What I need.

With guiding touches, I put his hand on my breast and tell him how I like to be caressed. How I enjoy it when my nipples are plucked and sucked upon, and Ossev is an eager student. He tends to my breast until my nipple is tight and aching, wet from his mouth, and then turns to the other one to give it the same care. As he does, his hand slips between my thighs, rubbing through my wetness, and begins to play with my clit.

He's a fast learner, my Ossev.

By the time he lifts his head for another kiss, I'm panting and hungry, on the verge of a climax. I moan as I grab a fistful of his silken hair and use my other hand to guide his cock into my body. We're gazing into each other's eyes when I seat myself upon him, and I don't know if I'm the one that gasps or if it's him. It doesn't matter. It feels amazing and connected and perfect.

I rock slowly on top of him, our mouths meeting in hungry, frantic kisses as our pace increases. When I whimper and think of how I need my clit to be touched to get off, his hand immediately moves back into action, his thumb rubbing over the perfect spot as I clench around him. Then I'm coming, hard and fast, clutching him tightly as I grind down on his length and he thrusts up into me.

The world ceases to exist outside of my labored panting and the sweaty clutch of our joined bodies. There's a low, contented throb deep inside me, and when I finally catch my breath and sigh, I realize Ossev has come, too. The insides of my thighs and my core are sticky with his release. He presses kisses on my bare shoulder, nuzzling my skin. "You've honored me," he murmurs. "My sweet Yulenna."

"*Our* sweet Yulenna," comes a voice from the doorway.

I'm not entirely surprised to turn and see Neska standing there. His silvery eyes are glittering, and he watches as I rock my hips over Ossev's softening length. Ossev tongues my nipple, biting down lightly upon it as I meet Neska's gaze, and I gasp with a new flutter of arousal. "It seems that Ossev is not the only one that likes to watch." My voice is shaky with tremors, even as Neska steps into the room, moving toward us. "Shall I call you naughty, too?"

"I am not naughty," he says in an imperious voice. "I am demanding."

He crosses the room to our sides and Ossev slips me off his lap, caressing my naked backside as he reclines back on the bed, watching as Neska stalks me and pulls me to him so he can kiss me in a fierce, possessive manner that I would have hated a few months ago and now makes me quiver with hunger.

Neska claims my mouth, biting down on my lower lip and making me whimper with need. He nips me hard and then licks away the flash of pain. "Have you been good to Ossev?"

I moan, because hearing the word "good" does something to me. "So good." I reach for him. "Did you watch?"

The thought makes me quiver deep in my belly. And even though I just climaxed, I know instinctively that they're not done with me. They never are after just one orgasm. They always want to give me more. And shamelessly, I will always *take* more.

He doesn't answer, but his gaze is unrelenting as he watches me press against him.

That's all right. I know the answer. "Did you like what you saw?"

"Yes and no." His gaze dips to my mouth. "I liked that you came. I did not like that it wasn't me."

"It can be you," I say, breathless. "I'm right here."

Before I can say anything else, he grabs me by the hips and pushes me up against the wall. Spiderwebs tangle into my hair as Neska covers my mouth with his, devouring me even as he slides his robe off. My arms go around him and we're kissing each other roughly, me biting his lip as he pushes between my thighs. He surges deep and I cry out with pleasure, clinging to him.

Neska takes me hard and fast, his breath heaving as he hammers into me with sharp, punching strokes. I'm slick from before, my body making wet, feverish noises as he claims me, but he doesn't seem bothered that I'm still wearing Ossev's leavings, or that the other Aspect remains on the bed, watching us. He's part of this, because we're all intertwined. The thought is an all-consuming one and it arouses me. I dig my nails into Neska's back, holding on tightly as he drives into me, and when I come, it's with a harsh, wrung-out cry in my throat and a climax that feels as sharp as a knife.

From the hiss that escapes him, I know Neska comes, too. His arms tighten around me and I slump forward from the wall, into his embrace. He holds me close, my legs locked at his waist, and brushes his lips over my cheek. "I liked that," he murmurs, just low enough for only me to hear. "Thank you."

I smile into his neck, sweaty and sated. "I am here to please you, my lord. All three of you."

"You do." He carries me over to the bed, laying me down beside Ossev's reclining form. "You always do."

Ossev reaches for my breast, squeezing it, even as Neska moves beside me, and I realize that again, we're not nearly done. They both touch me, their hands skimming over my skin. Neska kisses me, and when I turn my head, Ossev is there, his mouth as eager for me as the other. They play with my body until I'm whimpering with need again, and then Neska seats me atop his cock so I can ride him, and I jerk off Ossev, his release spraying over my skin while we kiss.

If Zaroun was here with us, this might be perfect.

Fourteen

Having two of the Spidae in my bed at the same time becomes the routine, and an exciting one. It seems that no sooner does one leave my side than he is replaced with another Aspect. Zaroun will spend hours in bed with me, touching me everywhere, and Ossev will join us. When Zaroun leaves, Neska will take his place, and then remain while I sleep. When I wake up, I will find both Zaroun and Neska with me in the middle, caught in a tangle of limbs.

They're not interested in touching each other. Their focus is solely upon me.

It's intense, too. I've had two lovers in my bed in the past, but never so regularly. The Spidae take care of me, though, ensuring that I'm never too tired for bedplay. I get plenty of naps and Apple brings me even more food than I can possibly prepare. Ossev helps me in my garden (well, he mostly stands around and looks perplexed when I dig in the dirt) and Zaroun bathes me and then rubs my shoulders.

I feel pampered and adored. Some people might find it overwhelming to have to satisfy three lovers, but it doesn't feel overwhelming to me. They're careful not to push me too hard, and when it's one of the rare days when I don't feel like touching or being touched—or I have my period—they hold me and we talk instead.

Neska especially frets when I have my period. He doesn't like it because it causes me pain and makes me tired. He tends to me carefully and even cuts up fruit for me when I don't want to get out of bed. The next month, my period doesn't come and I'm worried I'm pregnant.

"Not pregnant. I've stopped the cycle for you," is what Neska says when I ask. "I didn't like that it harmed you."

It *didn't* harm me, but I can't say I miss it. I've no desire to be a mother and being rid of a week of cramps and bloody discharge? It might be the greatest gift they've given me yet. They didn't ask me if I wanted it stopped, but I know how the three of them think now. They saw me hurting and strove to fix it. If I asked them to return it, the three of them would be confused why I'd want to ache for a week every month, but they'd do as I asked.

The mirror that allows me to look out onto the world and communicate with the other anchors soothes any anxiety I might have about being trapped here. I feel connected to others like me, and it lets me gossip with the others. When I get bored or restless, I can watch other people going about their lives and I'm reminded of how good I have it here, tucked away safe in the tower with three gods to watch over me.

Sometimes I use my mirror for other things, too.

I've been inspired by Ossev's proclivity for watching, and asked the mirror to show me a mortal couple in their bed. I watched for only a few moments, my breath in my throat, before Neska joined me. He pulled me into his lap and played with my pussy, rubbing me to release as he narrated naughty things into my ear and we watched the couple in the mirror. Since then, both Ossev and Neska have watched things with me, sometimes all three of us together. Perhaps I should feel a little guilty for intruding on someone else's privacy, but after the first time, I make sure that we find a couple that is in public in some way so I don't feel as if we're spying.

So yes...things in the tower are good. My garden blooms with plants, and though I don't have as much free time since I'm spending so much of my day with one of the three Aspects, I garden when I can. My sewing hasn't been as prolific, but I'm not too worried. I've got plenty of dresses and still find the time to stitch when I speak in the mirror with Faith (and now Max, Rhagos's anchor). We chat about everything and nothing, and I like having that outside connection, even if I feel no desire to leave the tower.

I'm quite content here.

Mostly.

There's only one small thing that makes me wonder...why are we not all three together? At once?

It bothers me, but they seem determined to avoid each other whenever possible. Unless someone is having sex with me, and then I will get a watcher who will eventually join in. But all three together in a room? Having a conversation? Spending time with each other?

Or all three of us in bed together? It never happens.

I tell myself that things are fine as they are, but it hangs over my head, a little cloud of doom reminding me that all is not perfect. That I am not serving all three of them, but each one individually.

It's not the same. It's either Neska and Zaroun together with me, or Zaroun and Ossev, or Neska and Ossev, but never all three. My bed is big enough for all of us, and I would love to share myself with all three of them at once, but it never seems to happen. At first I worried they were deliberately avoiding each other, but as I take two of them into my bed at once, I realize that's not the case.

Faith, the anchor to the Butcher God, is a very forthright woman. Perhaps she will have ideas for how I can approach this. I tap on my mirror, thinking of Faith, and wait to see if it will show me her face. Then, I sit down with my sewing to wait, pulling out the stitches on a complicated sleeve that ended up too tight.

"It's early," Faith declares with a yawn, appearing in the mirror. Her bright blonde hair is tousled and she rubs her eyes. "What's up?"

I glance out my window, eyeing the late afternoon sunlight. Time is fluid, I am reminded. Perhaps it is passing slower here. "I need advice. Are you too busy?"

"You need advice? From me?"

"Advice from one anchor to another," I agree, putting my sewing down for a moment.

"From...me?" She looks behind her as if checking to see if anyone else is in the room. "You do realize I'm with Aron, right? If anyone's doing it wrong, it's the two of us."

"But you are both happy," I point out. "Deliriously happy. He went to the Underworld to retrieve you from Rhagos's clutches."

"That was pretty baller," she agrees, a dreamy look on her face. "I'm going to have to remind myself of that the next time I want to choke him for being stubborn."

I twist my fingers in the soft fabric of the half-sewn sleeve. "I want to tell my lords Spidae that I wish for them to have dinner with me."

"Okay...?"

"All three of them. And then I should like for us to retire to bed together. All three of them."

Faith's brows go up. "O-kaaay. I'm not sure why you need advice from me on that sort of thing? Most guys are probably down with bookending. Or triple-ending. Or whatever. Stuffing holes, though I just cringed a little inside when I said that. You know what I mean. Why are you coming to *me* for this advice?"

I chew on my lip, worried. "I just...they are never together with me. It is never more than two of them in the room with me at the same time. I worry something is wrong. I worry they think I am too fragile to serve all of their needs at once. And I know I should be content that things have smoothed out, but I think I need *this*."

"Not something you hear every day," Faith says, tapping her finger on her cheek. "You really feel like you won't be complete unless you get all holes filled? I ask that as a friend."

I just give her a pleading look. "If you served two masters at once, wouldn't you want to serve both of them at once? At the same time? Sharing you in all ways?"

"Two Arons would probably destroy me, but I guess I can see it?" She spreads her hands. "If that's what you need to feel like you're doing your job for them properly, it's what you need. Here's a wild idea. Maybe try asking them instead of me?"

I hesitate, imagining this. Zaroun is half-lost in thought at all times. Neska is frequently jealous and overbearing. Ossev would be easy to ask, but he is only one side of our complicated triangle. "I don't know if it's as simple as that, my friend."

"You really think they could refuse you anything? Not to be crude, but have you tried asking on your knees?" She arches an eyebrow at me.

I laugh, because she has an excellent point.

Perhaps all I need to do is ask at the right time after all.

Fifteen

And so I ask.

Not on my knees. Discreetly, of course, so they don't feel something is upsetting me. When I get upset, all of them pace and get fussy.

I decide Ossev is the best one to approach, and so I wait until I'm in the garden one morning, pulling up a few weeds. Apple is at my side, pouncing on one of the rocks and then racing away again, and Ossev gazes at me as I kneel on a cushion, my hands in the dirt.

"Are you certain you enjoy this?" he asks, leaning over to watch me work. "I have watched humans tend to plants many times in the threads, but I do not yet grasp why shoving one's hands into the dirt brings feelings of pleasure."

"It's the satisfaction of a task completed," I tell him, tossing aside a long, slender weed. "Of taking something that's out of control back in hand once more. I like tending to my plants and knowing that they're taken care of. A bit like how the three of you like tending to me." Reaching down, I stroke one of the tiny leaves that have been slowly but steadily unfurling. "Speaking of the three of you, may I ask something?"

"Of course." His gaze is on my fingers, his expression mild, and I wonder that he can't guess at my thoughts. Are they quieter outside of the tower? It's an intriguing concept.

"Do you like sharing me with your other Aspects?" I sit back on my heels, brushing my fingers free of dirt.

"It does not bother me."

"But you do not touch each other."

He blinks up at me, gaze focusing on mine. "It does nothing for us. There is no pleasure to be found there. If Zaroun or Neska touches my hand, it is as if I am touching my own hand. I would much rather touch yours."

Interesting. I want to point out that self-pleasure can be very enjoyable, but if it's not something they are comfortable with, I won't press the issue. I can't help but notice that they call each other by the names I've given them, and that gives me a great deal of satisfaction. Perhaps they will eventually see themselves separately, as I see them. Linked but still unique. "I like you touching me," I say carefully, and then give him a suggestive smile. "I should like if all three of you touched me at once. Is such a thing possible? Can you leave your posts all at once?"

"Time is fluid," Ossev says, expression thoughtful. "If something urgent were to occur, we could hold it in place until we are there to observe and guide."

Is...that a yes? Or just him contemplating things? When he continues to give me a mild look, nudging at the dirt with one bare foot, I decide to prompt him again.

"Do I need to schedule time with the three of you?"

"Time is fluid," he says again, a puzzled expression on his face. "What are you asking?"

I sit back on my heels and clasp my hands in my lap, trying to seem composed and yet serious. "I would like for us to have dinner together." When his smile broadens, I clarify. "All three of you with me. Will that be a problem?"

"All three?" He tilts his head, as if confused.

"I am bound to all three of you," I say, continuing. "I want to establish that I am serving all three of you. I want to spend a lovely evening with dinner and conversation—again, with all three of you—and then I would like for us to go to bed together. All three of you. In bed. With me."

Ossev just blinks at me.

"Is that...doable? Or will that be a problem? I don't want to be selfish and cause issues with your webs, because I know your jobs are extremely important and take priority over my needs. But I would like that..." I brace myself, deciding to be firmer in my request. "No, I would love that. I *need* it."

"You need it?"

I nod again. It's hard to describe. How do I tell them that I need to serve all three of them at once to feel as if I'm truly filling my position? That I truly am their anchor? Right now I serve one of them at a time, or sometimes two. It doesn't feel as if we're all truly joined, as if we're all a cohesive unit. We feel like four separate units that sometimes pair up.

And I crave the intimacy of being possessed by all three of them at once. Of no one being left out or left wanting. It needs to be all of us, together.

I stare up at Ossev, these thoughts whirling in my head, wanting him to pluck them from my mind and understand it, to word it better than I can.

But he only gazes at me with a thoughtful expression, not moving. He's unnaturally still, not even a twitch to betray his thoughts. "You...wish to serve all three of us at once."

"In all ways," I agree, hoping I'm being clear enough. "In *every* way."

"And you would not feel...overwhelmed? By the presence of three gods in the same room with you?"

Is that what he worries over? "Not at all."

His gaze grows unfocused. "But how..."

Sometimes the Spidae are so very innocent, for all that they are immortal gods. I remind myself that they have said to me many a time that seeing something in the web does not mean comprehending it. "I have a mouth," I tell him. "I have two warm, wet holes. I have two hands. Surely between all of that I can manage to pleasure all three of you."

Ossev's gaze goes to my mouth and his eyes widen imperceptibly. I can almost see the flare of heat rising in his gaze, the fire inside him being stoked.

"You have not seen that in your webs, my lord?" I ask in a careful, soft voice.

"Yes, but it is not *you*. That makes it different. It is all different." He sounds astounded.

The High Father was wise to place me with them, then. There are so many things they understand and grasp now simply because I am here, because I am the mortal they are sworn to. It is as if I am the missing piece of the puzzle that stopped them from comprehending mortal relationships in all their ways. I wasn't sure at first that we could ever have a close relationship like I have seen with Faith and Aron of the Cleaver, but I know it is possible. We are almost there, all four of us.

"I would like to serve all three of you at once," I tell him. "*Please* let me serve you."

"When?" His voice is hushed, breathless.

"If it is possible for all of us to be in the same room and not cause distress to the webs, I should like to see you all tonight? We can have a lovely dinner and conversation. We can talk about how I can better serve all three of you." I clasp my hands over my heart. "And then we will go to bed together, if that pleases the three of you."

Ossev gives me a jerky nod. "Tonight."

"Shall I tell the others?"

"They know." He stares at my face, tilting his head in that strange way of his again, and then heads back into the tower.

I bite my lip, trying not to smile to myself. Tonight is going to be exciting. I must make myself ready.

I spend the rest of the day in preparations for that evening. If the Spidae are reading my mind, waiting for the right moment to arrive, I'm thankful. There's so much for me to do. I take a quick bath and pin my thick curls up so they won't get messy. Tonight is going to involve a great deal of oils and fluids, and I just washed my hair a few days ago.

Granted, I'll wash it again if it gets messy, but I'm a big believer in being prepared.

I dab a bit of scent at my pulse points and put on a new dress, one that's soft and flowing and made of a pale, pale chiffon in a delicate amber shade. My limbs are visible through the gauzy material when I walk, and it creates a pleasing tease to the senses. I put on a small corset to plump my breasts and show them off, and decide to skip both shoes and jewelry...and undergarments, but that is a given.

When I'm dressed and feeling sensual, I head down to the kitchens to prepare "our" meal. I know very well that the Spidae only eat if something intrigues them, so I cut up a few pieces of fresh fruit and then make myself a larger serving, adding nuts and a hard sweetbread I'm rather fond of. Several months ago, Apple brought me a bottle of wine with a label written in an unknown language, and I've been saving it for the right time. Tonight seems appropriate.

One more thing must be prepared for this evening, as well. I add herbs to a delicately-scented oil, thinking back to my days when I worked in a brothel. The girls there knew how to avoid infections, and this oil was a vital part of enjoyment, both for customers and for us.

Once the oil is steeping, the scent of it lingering in the kitchen, I maneuver the large table I have in the center of the stone floor, since I have no dining hall. I pour four glasses of wine, set out the four prepared plates, and then pull the two large, heavy chairs I have to the table, tossing a cushion on the hard back of each one so my lords can be comfortable. I add my only stool to the other side and then twist my hands, fretting.

I only have three seats, and they don't match. This feels wrong. I need another chair from…somewhere. But where? Racking my brain, I try to think of where I might have seen another chair in the tower. I have a large one near the fire in my room but getting it down the hall on my own seems impossible. Should I contact Neska or Ossev and ask one of them to move it?

A figure appears in the doorway. It's Neska, his silver eyes shimmering as he looks me over. Behind him, the other two god-aspects file into the room, and then all three of them are in the kitchen with me.

And…oh. Having all three of them in the same room feels strange. The air feels charged and heavy, and I'm very aware of the fact that they are gods and I'm a mere mortal. Is this why Ossev asked why I wanted all three of them together? Because it would feel overwhelming? Even so, I'm determined to see this through. I want this, and I don't care if I feel like a bug beneath their godly feet.

"Not a bug," Zaroun says in that dreamy, distracted way of his. "Mortal. Very different. Sweet. Tender. Soft. So mortal."

Right. Mortal isn't bad, just different, and it's because I'm mortal that I'm tied to them. Even so, I'm nervous, because I want tonight to be special. "I'm not ready," I protest, fluttering my hands over the table as they move into the room and join me. "Everything has to be perfect. Tonight is important—"

"You're ready," he says in that imperious voice of his. The god moves toward one of the large chairs, pulls the cushion off the back and tosses it to the floor.

I gasp, heat flooding my body at the sight of the pillow at his feet. It's been so long since I've sat on a pillow at anyone's feet, and it reminds me that sometimes serving a man can be *such* a pleasure. My hand flutters to my throat, because maybe I'm reading this wrong. "Does the chair not please you, my lord?"

"It does," Neska continues in that arrogant voice of his, his expression unreadable. "But it will please me more to have you sit at my feet."

And then he sits in the chair, elegantly resting his wrists upon the arms of it. His gaze is locked onto me, and I watch, heart pounding, as Ossev leads a blindfolded Zaroun to the other chair and then sits on the edge of the table, ignoring the place I've set for him. Their attentions are focused entirely on me.

"Ossev said he watched your threads," Neska says when I do not move. "That when you trusted a man in the past, you enjoyed serving him, sitting at his feet like a pampered pet. Or have we read this wrong?"

I swallow, trying to recall how long ago that was. A very long time, I think. Maybe ten years. I had an older client who was good to me, bought me gifts and took me out to fine dinners. How he'd wanted nothing except to spoil me, and so I felt comforted and safe around him. I'd loved kneeling at his feet and caressing his legs while he'd fed me tidbits, because when he was there, everything felt safe. Like he'd protect me from the world. I haven't thought of that man in ages, because he'd stopped coming to the brothel when he married, but I do remember the pillow at his feet and how I'd felt.

"It does take a lot of trust." I don't move just yet, because this is such a fine line and I want them to understand that there is a difference between submitting and serving because it brings you joy, and submitting and serving because you must. Part of me wants to sit on that cushion and part of me is afraid that if I do, we'll go back to the way things were. Where I'll be just a body for them to use and not think about beyond that.

"Then trust us," Ossev says, his gaze bright upon me. "Trust us to tend to your heart as well as your body."

Neska just waits, watching me. He sits, ramrod straight, his eyes narrow. He won't try to persuade me like Ossev will. He's going to make it my decision, my choice. I turn to Zaroun, because I can just ask him. I can ask what he sees if I climb onto that pillow, but that's not trust, is it? He turns towards me, his blindfolded face calm, waiting.

As I hesitate, Neska reaches out, palm up.

I slide my hand into his and sink onto the pillow, deciding to trust after all.

Sixteen

"Our sweet Yulenna," Neska murmurs, caressing my cheek with his knuckles as I settle against his legs. "We will not abuse your trust. Your heart is safe, now that we understand what a prize it is we hold."

There's a creak of wood, and then Zaroun moves his chair closer, his other leg brushing against mine. He leans forward, his long, spidery fingers stroking over my neck from behind. "So beautiful. So loving."

My eyes flutter closed and I enjoy this moment, being caressed and petted.

"Are you hungry, sweet Yulenna?" Neska's fingers glide to my mouth, tracing the edges of my lips. "Shall we feed you?"

I tingle all over, nodding.

"Ossev," Neska commands, and I'm not surprised to see him take charge when the three of them are in the room together. He's always been the one in control, hasn't he? "Feed our anchor. I want to watch."

Ossev hops off the edge of the table and moves to stand nearby, picking up a bit of fruit with his fingers. He considers it, then tosses it aside in favor of a different piece and then bends over, holding it out to me. "Open your pretty mouth."

It shouldn't feel nearly as carnal as it does to obey that simple command, but I open my mouth and display my tongue, waiting for the tidbit to be placed upon it.

Ossev murmurs approval, his fingers brushing against my tongue as he places a berry there. I eat it, letting the sweetness flood my mouth, and when Zaroun strokes my throat with long, slender fingers, just the act of swallowing somehow feels incredibly intimate. My hands creep up to Neska's leg and I hold onto him while Ossev feeds me another piece.

"Wine," Ossev declares. "She's thirsty."

"Wait." Neska sits up, and Ossev pauses. They both eye me. "You could spill something on her dress and she's worked so hard on it. I would not create more chores for our lovely anchor, not when she can be in bed with us instead."

My brows furrow as I watch this exchange that feels like it's for my benefit, and yet I'm not certain where they're going with this.

Then, Zaroun's hand slides down to the front of my bodice. He tugs at the strings, loosening it, and Neska is suddenly there, too, pulling the thick, stiff fabric of the corset free. Hands tug my dress down until my breasts are exposed to the air, the neckline of my dress bunched under my tits.

Neska caresses each one, thumb stroking over my nipples. "Better."

"Much better," Ossev agrees, and then holds another piece of fruit out for me.

Heat pulses through my center. This time, when Ossev feeds me a chunk of melon, the juice drips down my chin and Neska is there to catch the drops with his fingertips. Zaroun's hands move to my naked breasts, petting and stroking them, and a moan escapes me.

"I like this," Ossev says. "We should feed her like so every day."

"Perhaps we shall," Neska murmurs, his gaze locked on me. He feeds his wet fingertip into my mouth and I suck on it, hungry for more touches. "Would you like that, sweet Yulenna?"

"Yes." I tilt my head, rubbing my face against his hand. Right now I feel very pampered and adored, with their hands exploring me and their bodies looming over mine. "Please, my lords."

"I like it when you say that. You say it like we are yours."

"You *are*." I cling to Neska's leg, gazing up at him with hunger. "You are all three mine and I'm yours."

Zaroun flicks my nipple with a fingertip and I gasp, rubbing my face against Neska's hand again. "Feed her more," Neska demands. The Aspect of the Present flicks an imperious gesture at Ossev. "She needs her strength. Mortals must be fed regularly, and this one more than most because she serves three gods."

"I am," Ossev retorts. "Patience." He feeds another tidbit to me, and then gives me a crunchy nut, stroking my jaw when I chew. "Bread, and then wine."

I eat and drink obediently, curled up against Neska's legs. Zaroun continues to lean forward in his chair, stroking my exposed skin and caressing, as if he can't get enough of touching me. Ossev continues to feed me, taking great care to pick the best bites for me and then offering me small sips of wine to wash them down. This goes on for what feels like forever, until my stomach is full and my head is a little dizzy from the strong wine. I'm also floating because of their constant touches, each one sending heat pulsing straight to my core. Their nearness is overpowering, but it arouses me, too.

As Ossev lifts the cup to my lips for another sip, he tilts it slightly. It misses my mouth, spilling down my chin and onto my bare, exposed breasts. I gasp at the feel of the cool liquid on my heated skin, rearing back.

"Now our pretty pet is all dirty," Ossev murmurs. "We should fix that."

"Indeed. An excellent idea," Neska replies.

Then Zaroun's hands are sliding around my wet breasts, plumping them and pointing my nipples outward as his hot body presses up against mine from behind. I gasp again when Neska moves to the floor, licking at my wet skin. Ossev is upon my other breast in the next moment, lapping at my nipple.

Hot pleasure flashes through me. I whimper as they lick the wine from my skin, then keep on licking me. My world ceases to exist except for their hot, hungry mouths and Zaroun's gentle fingers holding my breasts for them. He nudges my cheek with his and I turn my head so we can kiss, our lips meeting hungrily even as another hand—Ossev's? Neska's?—slides under my dress and brushes over my drenched pussy.

"Should we retire to the bedroom?" Neska asks, lips still teasing my nipple. "Or shall we take her right here on the floor in the kitchen?"

I break from Zaroun's kiss and gaze down at him, our eyes meeting.

"Tell us how you want us, sweet Yulenna." His tongue flicks against my skin. "Tell us what you need. We are yours to lead."

Ossev's teeth scrape against my other breast, the sensation sharp, and it sends another hot curl of delight through my body. I stroke my hand through Ossev's hair as Neska waits for my answer, rubbing his face against the slope of my breast. They're waiting for me to say what I want, what I need. It occurs to me that I could end this now with a word and they'd honor it.

That even though I'm submitting to all three of them, I'm still the one in charge.

It's a heady, delicious feeling.

"I want all three of you at once," I say, just to put it out in the air. Just so there's no question of what my goal is. "I've got oil ready for us, so everyone is slick and it makes it easy on my body. Once we're oiled up, I think I'd like to go upstairs, to the bed. Please."

"Do you want us naked for your oil?" Ossev asks, nuzzling at the valley of my breasts. "Or is it just for you?"

"No, I'm going to put the oil on the three of you." I'm

breathless at the mental image. "And then you're going to oil me so I can take you in every way."

"Feels so good," Zaroun groans, as if I've already oiled him. His head dips against my neck, resting there.

I twine my fingers in Neska's hair, and when he kisses my breast again, I tug on it, forcing his head back. "Let me oil you, my lord. Let me oil all of you."

Ossev presses a kiss to my mouth before he stands, boldly undressing in front of my delighted eyes. He all but rips his belted sash from his hips—the one I made for him—and casts his pale robe aside. His long, otherworldly body is just as pale as the rest of him, but I've grown to love the spare, ethereal sight of the three of them, because I know that slender body holds a world of strength. His cock juts out, just as eager as the rest of him.

Neska is next to his feet, his silver gaze devouring me with its intensity. He carefully removes the sash I made for him and presses his lips to it in a tender gesture before setting it, folded, in his chair. Then he disrobes with the same meticulous movements, and when he's bared to my hungry gaze, his hand goes to his stiff cock, where a bead of webbing is already dripping from the head.

Zaroun slips from my side and puts his sash over his eyes, covering the existing blindfold, and smoothly and neatly drops his robe, then steps out of it.

All three of them are so beautiful and ethereal that it takes my breath away. This is a feast...and it's all *my* feast. Suddenly hungry to touch all of them again, I climb to my feet, my breasts swaying, and I pull my clothing off, too. I want to be just as bare as the three of them. I step forward, unable to help myself, and I love when their arms close around me. Hands brush all over my skin, caressing, and I kiss one before moving on to the next, making sure that I taste each one. Strangely enough, I can tell which one is which from scent and taste alone. Zaroun is mild, his taste sweet. Neska has just a hint of citrus to his scent, and Ossev is the most earthy of the three.

Neska captures my chin, turning me toward him again, and

his lovely silver eyes are hooded with arousal. "Your oil, pretty one."

Yes, of course. I've been distracted by their hands and mouths. I reluctantly pull away from their grasp and cross the room to get the bowl of oil. I fish the herbs out and breathe in the scent—it's steeped enough that it should be effective. Returning to my three lovers, I adore that their arms go around me, and yet when I'm not there, they seem to drift apart. "You can touch each other while I'm gone," I point out. "I won't mind. I'd find it sexy."

Ossev eyes Neska. Neska blinks at Ossev and glances over at Zaroun. The corners of Zaroun's mouth pull down with distaste.

"Or not. It doesn't matter to me." Perhaps it's something they'll like in time. Until then, I'm quite happy to greedily have them to myself.

I give the bowl to Ossev and dip my fingers into it, then reach over to stroke Zaroun's cock with glistening hands. He groans, his body shuddering under my touch, and reaches for me. I let him touch me for a time, kissing him as I work his shaft, and then pull away. His hands trail over my back as I dip my fingers again, this time moving to Neska. The look he gives me is almost challenging, but when I lean in for a kiss, he cradles my face in his hands and reverently kisses me back. When I move to Ossev, Neska makes a noise of pure frustration, but he doesn't stop me. I oil up Ossev too, my hands moving over his gorgeous cock and stroking it with slick, confident motions. I can't help but reach for Neska again, and then I'm jerking both of them off while they touch me, my breath catching in my throat.

Zaroun kisses my shoulder, slipping behind me. "Now you, pretty one."

Ossev's eyes flare with anticipation and he sets the bowl of fragrant oil on the table, slicking his fingers as Neska runs a hand down my front. They touch me with gentle caresses and kisses until I'm quivering, and then Ossev's greased fingers are skimming over my pussy.

"She's so hot and wet already," he says aloud. "Feel her."

Neska drags his fingers through the bowl of oil and then touches me, his fingers competing with Ossev's for dominance. I whimper as they touch me in tandem, hands moving over my clit and my folds, then stealing into my aching channel. My knees buckle and I lean weakly against Zaroun as they touch me, over and over, the only sound that of my ragged breathing and the whisper of my name on their lips.

"She is slick now," Neska says, speaking up. "Turn her, Zaroun, so we can oil her other hole."

And even though this was part of my plan, and I've been anticipating it from the start, I can't help the whimper of need that escapes me. Zaroun's arms are around me, his mouth on mine as he kisses me into distraction. Ossev runs slick hands up and down my flanks, then presses between my thighs, demanding that I spread wide for them.

I do, and immediately their hands are there, teasing and stroking my cunt. I make a choked sound against Zaroun's mouth, clenching against their invading fingers. It feels so intense that I want to shimmy away…and I want to bear down on them at the same time. A hot mouth presses kisses to my buttock even as fingers press against the pucker of my backside. Burying my hands in Zaroun's hair, I cling to him as even more fingers push into my ass.

"Touch her, Zaroun," Neska is saying. "Feel how tight and hot she is back here."

And then Zaroun is abandoning me, too. I bend over, helpless, as all three of them stretch and tease the entrance to my ass, preparing it for further invasion. The sensation of all three of them touching me like this is as stark as it is delicious, and the only reason I don't fall over is because there's a tight arm locked around my waist, holding me up.

"Spread her wide," Neska commands. "Look at how good she takes all three of us. So very pretty, our anchor. So very willing, too."

I moan. "Bed. Now. Please, my lords."

A finger rubs in and out of my ass, teasing, but then they're all slipping away and I'm being peppered with kisses once more. "Are you ready for us?" asks Ossev.

"All three of us?" Zaroun nips at my shoulder.

"In all of your pretty holes, sweet Yulenna?" Neska grips my hips and rubs his cock against the cleft of my backside, and it sends a bolt of sheer yearning through me.

I nod, beside myself with need. All I know is that I need more than teasing touches from the three of them. I need *everything*.

"Bed," someone says, and I don't know who it is.

In the next moment, the room shifts and shimmers and then we're upstairs, the edge of the mattress touching my knees. I stagger forward, hands planting against the center of the bed.

"Look how eager she is," Neska purrs. A hand strokes down my back, cupping my ass. "She's hungry for all of us."

"Yes," I agree. "Please."

It's true. I can't wait for more. I need this like I need air.

But when no one reaches for me, I whimper a needy protest and turn around to face them. "I want to be with all three of you, my lords."

Zaroun is still as a pillar. Ossev isn't looking at me, but at Neska. The silver-eyed fate blinks once, but is otherwise still. "Patience, sweet mortal. We are convening."

Convening? Are they having an argument over who gets to touch me first? Are they arguing in their minds? *Now?* When I'm so needy and close to an intense climax? Their timing is terrible. Fine then. If they need convincing, I'm happy to apply my skills to do so. I sink to my knees in front of Neska, taking his slippery cock in my mouth and sucking on him eagerly. He tastes like oil and herbs, but it's not an unpleasant taste. It's one that makes me think of sex, and I moan even as I take him deep into my throat, one hand wrapped around the base of his shaft.

He makes a startled sound, and a hot, salty splash hits the back of my throat. I keep sucking on him, reaching for the closest person as I do. It's Zaroun, and when I caress his cock, he eagerly moves forward so I can touch him better.

"She did tell us she was eager," Ossev says, stroking a stray hair back from my face. There's a tone of approval in his voice. "Take charge, Neska. Tell us where we should be to pleasure her the most."

I quiver, my pussy clenching tight at the thought. I like how he phrases it, too. It's not "tell us where we can get off" but "tell us where we can give Yulenna the most pleasure." It makes me feel like I'm in control even though there's three gods to one mortal.

"Zaroun," Neska manages, even as I bob my head over his cock. He's still leaking into my mouth and showing no signs of softening. I know from experience that he can come repeatedly without flagging, so I hollow my cheeks and keep sucking even as I gaze up at him.

Zaroun's breath catches, my hand moving over his slippery length. Without lifting my head, I reach for Ossev, too. He's only too happy to press his shaft into my seeking hand, and then I've got all three of them at once. The same charged energy that fills the room seems to float through me, sending prickles of delight through my body and making my nipples tighten. I moan around Neska's cock.

"Shh, shh," he tells me. "Patience. We will make it worth it."

My eyes flutter shut, loving the sweet, doting tone of voice he uses as he cups my chin. Gods, but I love putting my guard down enough to serve.

"Eyes open," he tuts, tapping my cheek. "Part of the pleasure is the watching, yes? I know you like to watch."

I whimper, because it's true.

Neska pins me in place with his intense silvery gaze. His cock feels enormous in my mouth, and it takes everything I have to keep my jaw slack so I can keep him in place. Saliva pools at the corners of my mouth and leaks down my chin. I'm a mess. But Neska only smiles at the sight, as if the knowledge that I'm losing control just to suck on him pleases him greatly.

"Do you want her ass, Ossev?"

My hand involuntarily squeezes around his cock, and Ossev strokes my hair, groaning. "You know I do."

"Then Zaroun will lie upon the bed and our sweet Yulenna will mount him and take his cock into her cunt. When she's settled upon him, you will mount her from behind and please her that way."

Oh gods. My pussy clenches around nothing, and I feel so empty and aching. How I want this.

"And you?" Ossev asks.

"I like where I am." He smiles down at me, the look that of a controlling master, and it nearly makes me come. "She can keep suckling me, can't you, sweet mortal?"

I manage to nod even as he pushes deeper into my mouth, eager to please.

"Good girl," he breathes, and I swear my pussy gets even wetter.

Zaroun's hands stroke up my arm, and then all three of them are pulling me to my feet. I make a sound of protest as I lose Neska's cock and it slides out of my mouth, gleaming wet and glossy with saliva and oil. I no longer have my hands on their cocks, either, and I reach for bodies, desperate to touch so they'll touch me back.

"Patience," Neska chides again, wiping the oil-slick corners of my mouth. "Or you will not get what you desire."

I don't think they'd deny me at this point, but I love the dominant edge of Neska's voice. There's something so freeing about trusting him with my pleasure enough to let him be the demanding, particular deity that he is. That he can be who he is best and focus all of that controlling nature on my pleasure as much as his own.

He strokes his thumb over my lower lip. "Would you like to sit on Zaroun's face, Yulenna?"

"Yes," I plead. My aching pussy would love that.

"If you're good, then you can do that later when I am in your ass," Neska murmurs. "But for now, you get Zaroun's cock."

Hands reach for my hips, and I realize Zaroun is laying down upon the bed, waiting for me. Oh. I don't want Zaroun to feel left out of anything because he's not as demanding as the other fates, so I lean over him and kiss him passionately, showing him how much I adore him with my mouth, and how he's just as important to me as the others.

"I know," he whispers, nipping at my swollen lips. "Always know."

I continue kissing him, even as I slide my hips over his and rock against his cock. I love the stutter of his breath against mine, and how his hands grip me tightly with need. I reach between us, feeding him into my achingly empty cunt, and moan against his lips when I finally sink down upon his shaft. "Gods, that's good."

"Tell us how she feels, Zaroun," Neska says, his hand gliding down my spine and then teasing my ass. "Is she tight and wet and clenched around you?"

I moan at his words at the same time Zaroun does.

"Perfect," Zaroun manages. "Our Yulenna...always so perfect."

His flattery makes me feel like the most sensual woman ever. I rock my hips atop him, driving him deeper into me. I love the friction between our bodies, and the way he grunts and rises to meet me.

"Ride him," Neska commands, stroking my cheek. "Ride him but don't let him come yet."

Tease him? Oh, I can absolutely tease Zaroun. I brace my hands at his sides and move nothing but my hips, bouncing up and down atop his cock. The sensation of his thick shaft shuttling inside me is so good that I bite my lip, focusing on my own pleasure. I could squeeze out a small climax, then—

Neska's fingers tighten on my chin. "Not yet, impatient one."

I whine at him, moving faster on Zaroun, riding him with all the hunger and need in my body. My pussy is *so* slick and his cock feels so good that I can feel the climax just drifting out of reach. I need it so badly that everything inside me aches with wanting.

"She's greedy," Ossev says, running a hand down my back. The bed shifts as he climbs in behind my working hips. "Look at how hungry she is to come."

"Our naughty anchor can wait," Neska replies, and lifts one of my hands from the bed.

I moan a protest, sinking back on Zaroun's rigid shaft, only for my other hand to go into the air, too. It takes me a moment to realize that he's using webbing as ropes, tying my hands in place.

I jerk against the bonds, gasping, and Neska catches my chin again. He cups it, and looks deep into my eyes. I quiver, clenching around Zaroun's cock as I stare at Neska and his expression of pure control.

"Do you want to stop?"

Panting, I shake my head. "No, my lord."

"If you want to stop, you have but to think it." He studies my face, then leans in and gives me a surprisingly gentle kiss. "We will know when you are no longer enjoying yourself, pretty one. You are safe with us."

I'm touched that he's reassuring me...touched and frustrated that he's distracted me away from my orgasm. "I know."

And then I move my chin, biting down on his thumb.

He growls low in his throat, his eyes gleaming, and I can tell he's pleased by my "naughtiness." "Claim her ass, Ossev. Fill her up and remind her that she's not in charge."

A hand spreads on my lower back, tilting me forward, and I moan again.

"That's right," Ossev murmurs, his other hand spreading my ass cheeks and pressing his thumb against the back entrance to my body. "Be a good girl and we'll make you come."

Zaroun gasps when I clench around him at Ossev's words.

"She likes being called a good girl," Neska points out. "Did you feel how she tightened around him?"

"Perhaps she just likes my finger in her arse," Ossev murmurs, moving closer. I can feel the heat of him pressing against my back.

"B-both," Zaroun manages. "She likes both."

I want to protest that I can answer for myself, but they're not wrong. I do like this. Too much. It's distracting and delicious and I can feel my body tensing, desperate to release with an orgasm. I tug on the bonds on my wrists but they hold tight, and it adds another layer of salaciousness to things—that I'm unable to get away no matter how hard I try.

The head of Ossev's cock rubs against the pucker of my ass and I moan, anticipating the hard thrust that will come next.

It doesn't, though. Instead, his hand steals around to my front and rubs my clit, fast and furious, and I climax hard, crying out with my release. He keeps rubbing, wringing the release from my body even as Zaroun makes ragged sounds underneath me. By the time I finish climaxing, I'm limp, wrung out and exhausted as I hang in the webs from my arms.

Ossev leans in and kisses my shoulder. "She needed that."

"Well, we'll just have to make her come again," Neska replies, and he sounds a little miffed that Ossev took control.

"Oh, we will." Ossev rubs his thumb in and out of my greased backside, and I let out an exhausted little moan as he does. A moment later, it's not his thumb there but his cock once more, and when he presses me forward again, Zaroun's arms go around me. My arms are straight out to my sides and I whimper as Zaroun's hands move lower, spreading my ass cheeks so Ossev can push his way into my body.

It's been a long, long time since I've taken two lovers at once, and I've forgotten how invasive and tight it can feel. Like I'm being pushed to the limit of what my body can handle. I whimper as Ossev feeds his cock deep inside me, working slowly but steadily. Neska continues to stroke my face, murmuring filthy words about how deep Ossev is going into my ass, how good it looks to see me filled so fully, how Zaroun feels when my cunt tightens with every breath.

Ossev taps my ass cheek, making it jiggle, and then he gives a grunt of pleasure, leaning heavily over me. "So good."

"Yulenna?" Neska asks.

I'm dimly aware of his hand on my chin through the haze of pleasure. My legs feel spread wide, Ossev's cock invading deep into me and my cunt clenching over and over around Zaroun's as he lies beneath me, his hands stroking over my front. It almost feels like too much, but when I meet Neska's gaze, I realize that I still want more.

I want Neska, too.

So I open my mouth wider and give him a pleading look.

"Do you want me, too?" he asks, his gaze intense on mine. "You don't have enough yet, greedy girl?"

"I have a mouth that has yet to be filled, my lord."

He chuckles, but I can see the way his eyes flare that he likes this. He likes being asked to join. He likes being in control even though the focal point of our twined bodies is my pleasure, not theirs.

"Do you think you can take me without your hands?" he asks, tilting his head even as the others begin to move against me. I moan, because it's like being dragged along with the tide. All I can do is hold on for the ride as both Ossev and Zaroun grip me and thrust. All the while, Neska holds my chin in place, forcing me to look him in the eyes. "I like the sight of you tied up too much to let you down."

"I can take you, my lord," I promise. "Let me show you."

Ossev's hand steals to my shoulder and he's holding me in place as he rams into my backside with swift, firm strokes that make my breath hitch. Zaroun is gentler, but no less eager. Then Neska is there, not standing on the bed but next to it, webbing under his feet and lifting him off the ground so he's at the perfect height for me to suck him off.

I take him into my mouth eagerly, hot pleasure rolling through me. This is what I've wanted all along—all three of my

Spidae here in the bedroom with me. All three of us connected and loving together.

"All three of us here with you," Neska agrees, sinking a hand into my hair as I take him into my throat and work him with my mouth. "Together."

Zaroun shudders underneath me, a hot stickiness spilling down the insides of my thighs with his release. If anyone is disappointed at how quickly Zaroun has climaxed, it doesn't show, because he continues to stroke inside me, his movements becoming more frantic, and I realize he's going to come more than once. Ossev grunts and holds onto me tighter, even as I continue to tongue Neska. I suck on him hard, and he groans and pulls from my mouth just before he comes, spraying webbing over my chin and my breasts. Zaroun fills me again, our bodies making slick noises as he drives into me, and he glides his thumb over my clit, ensuring that I come a second time, too.

Ossev is the last to climax, and when he does, he pulls out and covers my backside with his release, my skin sticky and marked from all three of them. I hang limp in the webbing, sagging in place as Ossev rests against my back and Zaroun pants underneath me. Neska remains standing, but he pulls me against him, stroking my now-unbound hair and resting my cheek against his belly.

The air still feels charged with energy from the three of them, but it's less intense, less urgent. It feels...sated.

I lift my cheek from Neska's stomach, webbing sticking to my skin and connecting the two of us. He continues to caress my face lovingly, even as I focus on the tangle of our limbs. Everywhere, there's webbing. It's splattered all down my front and runs in rivulets down the insides of my thighs. My backside feels covered, too. When I look over at Neska, his midriff is spattered with strands, and Zaroun looks almost as messy as I do.

The bedding is going to have to be washed thoroughly, several times, I think.

"Was that what you wanted, sweet anchor?" Neska asks,

caressing me again. The fiery intensity is gone from his gaze, and his expression is downright doting. "Have we pleased you?"

I nod happily. For me, it wasn't about climaxing. It was just about feeling connected to the three of them at the same time. The fact that they made me come twice—and that they each came, too—is just added pleasure. "It was everything I wanted."

One of them reaches out and frees one arm, and then the other, and I collapse and roll onto the bed with Zaroun. He immediately slides his arms around me, turning on his side and pillowing his head on my face. I touch his cheek, mindful of the blindfold, and I'm pleased when Ossev moves to my other side, spooning against me. Neska moves onto the bed too, lying near our heads and stroking my hair as he does. We'll have to get up in a moment to clean up, but for now, I'm surrounded by the press of bodies and webbing and I couldn't be more content.

Gazing up at the ceiling, I notice the ever-present webbing there, too. A new thought occurs to me and I giggle to myself. Is that why there's spiderwebbing all over the tower? I have a sudden, wild mental image of each of the Spidae clutching their cocks in hand, spraying the walls with their seed.

"Naughty thing," Ossev murmurs, pressing a kiss to my shoulder. "You'd like that, wouldn't you?"

"Only if she gets to watch," Neska adds, and even as I chuckle, my mind floods with more lewd, spiderweb-covered ideas.

Perhaps I'm a naughty thing after all. But I'm *their* naughty thing, and that's the best part.

Epilogue

My garden is beautiful.

Well...it's not truly *my* garden. Mine died on the first bitter day of weather and nothing grew bigger than a seedling no matter how hard I tried. I fretted about it for what felt like months, but then my sweet Spidae lords called in a favor for me. Lord Kassam, God of the Wild, went to work upon the sad remains of my garden and created a wonderland. Now, it is lush and beautiful and immune to any rogue weather, with fruit hanging from every vine and bough.

I wander through the greenery, caressing huge leaves as I do. I breathe in the scent of a flower, in full bloom despite the grayness of the day, and feel very loved indeed. I touch several of the flowers before I select one to cut for my table, and then move down to the large cucumbers growing on vines on the ground. I choose a small one for my snack, and then head inside with my treats. My magical, god-touched garden grows so very quickly and plentifully that I have to prune regularly, but I don't mind. Apple helps me, and when it's too much food even for me, I bind it in a cocoon and send it to the other anchors, Faith and Max.

Carly—the wild god's anchor—doesn't need gifts of fruit, I imagine. I send her pretty dresses instead.

Ossev is waiting for me in the doorway that leads to the tower, and I smile up at him. "Cucumber tonight."

He wrinkles his nose, considering, as I move past him in a sweep of bright red skirts. "Have I had this kind yet?"

"You had it pickled," I point out. "This is fresh. I'll add a bit of salt to bring the flavor out and it'll taste different, you'll see."

"Then I will taste it again."

I beam at him, amused. A cucumber isn't a meal, of course, but the things I add to my plate—dried meat, nuts, and bread—don't appeal to him. He's my nibbler, Ossev. He likes to try everything in the garden just because he sees me eating it and doesn't want to miss out on a bit of pleasure. Zaroun is easy to please, and Neska likes things he's familiar with, but Ossev has the most adventurous palate out of the three. I do my best to change up things so he can try new treats regularly.

We've settled into a routine that is both comfortable and enjoyable. I think some anchors might want a life of excitement and thrills, but I love that the tower is mine and that I have everything I should want. I have no desire to leave or abandon my three lords. If I find myself on the rare occasion bored or restless, there's always a mirror to gaze into...or I can use it to contact my friends. Faith and I talk regularly, Max and Carly less so. It's nice to have a circle of companions that understand what it's like to serve a god, though. It's even nicer to be able to talk to those friends from the comforts of my tower room.

Ossev plants a kiss on my cheek and caresses my backside through my skirts. "Neska is looking for you."

"I haven't gone anywhere." I'm amused that Ossev is here to relay the message and not Neska himself. The Fate of the Present is the most prickly of the three, quick to sulk if he feels he doesn't get his share of my time. It's a constant push-pull between us for control of the relationship, but I always win. Neska wouldn't share me at all if he had his choice, but I've made it clear that I'm here for all three of them, not just him.

And because the three of them make me happy, he goes along

with it. We don't all three get into bed together often—they're still happiest having me to themselves—but when we do, it's explosive and exciting.

"Yes, but Neska says he has something important to speak with you about." His arms go around me from behind and then Ossev is hugging me. "You should talk to him."

This isn't like Ossev. He's not clingy like Zaroun. If anything, he's the most playful out of the three. His mood seems to be off and that worries me. Has he seen something bad in his threads? Another war? Now that Aron of the Cleaver has returned to his plane, he's been quick to start more conflicts, and sometimes I feel the reverberations of those in my Spidae's moods.

"What is it?" I ask Ossev, curious.

"Just...speak to Neska."

I nod, putting aside my cucumber to eat later. I'm hungry, but I'm always hungry as the anchor to three gods. Food can wait for a little while. Ossev's insistence and his strange mood is worrying me. "Let me tell Zaroun I'll be late. I'm supposed to spend this afternoon with him."

We kiss and I study his face, trying to determine what's wrong. It can't be war. They get agitated when there's war, but not worried like this. Ossev's touch lingers as I step away, as if he can't bear to let me go, and I think about that even as I climb the ramp up the tower towards Zaroun's web chamber.

The Aspect of the Future is there, waiting for me as always. His back is to me, his hands buried in the glowing strands as he sorts through them, pulling them from the weave and pinching them free when necessary.

"Zaroun?" I call out, waiting by the doorway. "I am here."

He turns, his eyes closed, and a smile curves his face as he steps in my direction. "Yulenna?"

"It's me." I move toward him, touching his arms when I'm close enough. "I must visit Neska before I return. Do you know what that's about?"

"All will be well...?" He tilts his head in that spiderlike way they do sometimes.

"Is that a question? Are you asking me?" I chew on my lip, anxious.

"Will it be well?" Zaroun touches my cheek. "Yulenna is happy. All well."

He doesn't know the answer, then. He doesn't know what this is about, and that worries me. Zaroun's words get confusing when he tries to explain things he can't see clearly. Whatever this is, though, it's about me. Have I done something to offend Neska, I wonder. I think of last night, when I sat at his feet and he fed me tidbits, and then he lapped at my pussy until I came three times. Then he had Ossev fuck me while I had my head in Neska's lap and sucked his cock. I had a lovely time and we'd curled up in bed together afterward, so I thought he'd enjoyed that, too. I don't think he left upset, but perhaps something else is wrong?

"I'll return shortly, I promise," I tell Zaroun.

"All well," he says softly, a sad look on his face.

Tears prick at my eyes and I blink them away, frustrated and worried. It makes no sense to weep when I don't even know what's wrong. But I don't like the sadness and concern in Ossev and now Zaroun. I all but race up the ramp towards Neska's chambers, my heart pounding in my breast.

He's there, standing apart from his strands and staring at them thoughtfully. When I enter the room, he turns toward me, and his expression is typical Neska—completely unreadable.

"What's going on?" I ask, storming in, my rustling skirts catching around my legs as I rush forward. "Ossev told me to come here and Zaroun is being distant. Why is everyone acting so strange? You're worrying me."

Neska gazes down at me for a long moment. Normally when he stares down at me like that, he reaches out and touches my face or strokes my mouth. He loves to stroke my mouth. Today, though, he doesn't reach for me, and that worries me as much as anything.

"I—*we* have been conferring with the High Father."

My eyes go wide. The High Father?

Neska's silver eyes are slitted, emotionless. "He feels we are sufficiently connected with humanity again and have learned a great deal. Your presence is no longer required. You can leave at any time."

I stare up at him in surprise. I thought anchors to gods served for life? I thought they enjoyed me being their anchor? I thought... "Oh."

His face is unreadable. "Tell me where you wish to be dropped—and *when*—and it shall be done."

"Oh..." I fight back another sudden rush of tears. I've had this before—getting settled and comfortable only for my life to be turned upside down once more. For the man (or men) that I serve to grow tired of me. So why does it hurt so much this time? Why does it feel as if my heart has turned to ice?

I've grown fond of the three Spidae. I adore them and love how they treat me. I love my home here in the tower. I love my garden. I love Apple, my strange, playful spider. I love the mirror I have that allows me to spy on everyone, and I love having an endless supply of cloth for pretty dresses. I love being safely tucked away from the cruel world with them and not having to worry about where my next food—or my next client—might be.

Most of all, I love the Spidae. I love Ossev for his curiosity and eagerness. I love Zaroun for his sweetness and spending quiet time with him. I love Neska in his controlling, intense ways and how he demands and acts as if he wants to conquer me...and if I have so much as a splinter, he's the first to fuss and get upset over my pain. They make me feel special and cherished, and I love each one of them individually and also as a whole.

I can't see my life without them in it. I can't see myself going back to Rastana, or Aventine, or even the eastern kingdoms. I want to stay right here.

But I might not have that option. "I...see."

"You are very quiet."

"I don't know what to think," I answer honestly. Dropping my gaze, I notice his hand twitches at his side, then flexes. It's like he wants to touch me but doesn't trust himself.

That small move makes me pause. I think about Ossev, and Zaroun's disjointed words about me being happy. Are they doing this for me? Giving me the choice so I can be free?

I glance up at Neska. "Do you want me to stay?"

He swallows, the movement strangely human. His gaze flicks over me. "I...will not influence you."

But there's a hitch in his voice that betrays him. I know him well enough to recognize that. When Neska is in his element, he is all sharp words and cutting statements. For him to hesitate tells me everything.

So I take his hand and bring it to my cheek, and I feel his fingers twitch against my skin. "Do you want me to stay, my lord? Yes or no?"

"I want what will bring you happiness." His fingers tremble and then smooth over my cheek. "The choice should be entirely yours."

"But you're upset. All three of you are. I can tell." I turn my face, pressing into his palm and kissing him there. "It's a very human thing, to be upset at a time like this. The High Father was right. You have learned a lot."

"If you want your freedom, we would not keep you. Your misery would not bring us happiness." His hard mouth draws up at the corners in a tiny smile. "I hate that I realize that now."

"Because you care for me? It's not a bad thing to care. It makes you better at your work. It makes you sympathize with mortals. I'm glad of it, even if it troubles you." I smile up at him, touched. "And I like that you worry over how I feel."

He's silent.

I don't mind his silence. I know it's because he's feeling a lot in this moment. His actions tell me everything. The small twitches of his hand. The way he stares at me as if he could burn holes into my gown. I move forward, skimming a hand down the front of his white silken robe and pause at the sash at his waist. He's wearing the one I made him.

He always wears the sash, even though I've fussed over some of the messy stitches and offered to redo it for him. He wears it faithfully every day. "You've got your sash on."

"Always. It is my most treasured possession."

I glance up at him, smiling at his sweetness. "You know, Neska...I understand that you don't want to keep me if I don't want to be here. I appreciate the offer. But if it makes you feel any better, you couldn't keep me if I wanted to go."

He practically bristles at the playful tone of my voice, and I have to fight back amusement. "I could absolutely keep you."

"No, I assure you, you could not. If I didn't want to stay, I wouldn't."

Neska's eyes narrow. "What if I tied your hands and feet with webbing?"

I pretend to consider, then playfully answer, "I'd orgasm so hard that I'd never want to leave anyhow."

He huffs with amusement, but some of the tension eases from his long, slender form. "You orgasm quickly as it is."

"I do. My three lords know just what I like to make me come." I trail my fingers over his chest. "They know how to please me in bed...but they don't know how to ask me if I want to stay with them or not. Curious, don't you think?"

Neska tenses under my hand. "You...wish to stay? To remain as our anchor?"

"More than anything. I love being yours. I love that the three of you belong to me. I never want to leave."

His eyes blaze with warmth, and the tension leaves the air. He reaches for me, cupping my cheek and then my neck, and pressing his forehead to mine. "You're certain?"

"Completely. I love being your anchor...the anchor for all three of you."

He makes an amused sound in his throat. "You are the only

person in the universe that sees us as three separate faces instead of one with three facets."

"Then I'm the only one you need." I smile up at him, full of relief. "At least until I grow old and you tire of me."

"No. Never." He shakes his head, eyes closed, forehead still pressed to mine.

"I'm mortal. We age—"

"No."

That makes me pause. He's so certain. "No...?"

"We made a deal with Rhagos. Death will never touch your thread. As long as you are ours, you will never age, either. That is something we control." He traces my ear with a fingertip. "You will be just as frozen in time as we are. Does that bother you? What do you think?"

"I think...it gives us a lot of time to cover the walls with spiderwebs." I grin up at him. "Lots and lots of spiderwebs."

Neska just groans and then he's kissing me. My heart is full. I kiss him back, showing him how much I love him. I'm not surprised when other hands caress my back, touching me and letting me know that the other two Spidae have arrived. We share this moment of pure unadulterated joy.

It will be the first of many, I suspect, because time is long... and we have as much of it as we want.

Author's Note

Hello there!

Ever since *Bound to the Battle God* came out, I've had people asking for Yulenna's story. Everyone wanted to know more about the woman who selflessly offered herself up to three weirdos (hah). While I thought Yulenna definitely had a story, it seemed like more of a novella than a full-length novel to me. Most of the Aspect and Anchor books are hugely long and epic in scope, and Yulenna's story would more or less be confined to the tower itself, because the three Spidae never leave it.

The more I thought about it, the more I thought there might be more to their story. The Spidae present themselves as the same to the outside world, but I couldn't help but think of how each job handled by each aspect would affect them. Ossev (the past) is a watcher and a bit of a gossip. Neska (the present) is controlling. Zaroun (the future) is slightly melancholy. I wanted to explore this a bit and how they related to Yulenna, and it ended up being a lot of fun—and spicy!

(Speaking of spice - this might be the spiciest in the series? But you can't have a woman with three men and NOT get them all in bed at the same time. I mean, come on. And as for the streams not crossing...I felt the Spidae's relationship came across as a little too familial as it is, and so for them to touch each other would not be a natural inclination. Like Yulenna said, she'll have to work them into it in the future.)

I've picked at this story for a while now — every time I started it, another deadline would jump ahead. Those that follow me on FB know that I've been working on it for a while, so I'm doubly elated to have it completed because I know you've all been waiting on it! I'm so thrilled that you finally get to read about Yulenna and Ossev, Neska, and Zaroun. I've more ideas for this world in particular, with at least two of them in my 'idea' pile so look for more announcements in the future! I particularly want to get to Kalos, the God of Disease. He seems like he'd be fun at parties.

A special thank you to Zintle Mfobo for being my sensitivity reader. Your notes were absolute perfection and I'm glad you loved this quartet as much as I did!

<3
Ruby

Want More?

Want more of the Aspect and Anchor world? Just want more Ruby Dixon in general? All of my books are in Kindle Unlimited, so borrow away!

The Aspect and Anchor Series
Bound to the Battle God
Sworn to the Shadow God
Wed to the Wild God

Also in the same universe
The King's Spinster Bride
The Half-Orc's Maiden Bride

Ruby Dixon Backlist

Enjoy!

Printed in Great Britain
by Amazon

47508945R00098